Happy Birthday, Dear Darrell

and Other Stories

Happy Birthday, Dear Darrell

and Other Stories

ROBERT LACY

STEPHEN F. AUSTIN STATE UNIVERSITY PRESS

IBSN: 978-1-62288-207-6

For more information:
Stephen F. Austin State University Press
P.O. Box 13007 SFA Station
Nacogdoches, Texas 75962
sfapress@sfasu.edu
www.sfasu.edu/sfapress
936-468-1078

Distributed by Texas A&M Consortorium
www.tamupress.com
Book Design: Ben Adams/Jerri Bourrous

Contents

Acknowledgments

Most of these stories were previously published as follows:

"Win a Few, Lose a Few" in *The Saturday Evening Post*

"Occurrence at 133 Park Street, Apartment 2A" in *Carolina Quarterly*

"Happy Birthday, Dear Darrell" in *Crescent Review*

"Everyone Asked About You" in *Great River Review*

"Second Wives" in *Antioch Review*

"Incident at Camp Matthews" in *Sewanee Review*

"Samaritan" in *North Stone Review*

"Hooray for Hollywood" in *Press*

"Three-Hundred and Twenty-Six Jackrabbits" in *North Dakota Quarterly*

Also, earlier versions of "Everyone Asked About You" and "Second Wives" appeared in *The Natural Father, New Rivers Press*, 1997.

Win a Few, Lose a Few

The unchallenged high point of every school year at Mansfield Junior High was the assembly period on the day the football lettermen were announced and called forward to receive their green and gold sweaters. The moment held real drama, because in separating its wheat from its chaff, Mansfield, like most other schools in this particular state, employed a single pitiless measure: those sweaters. A boy got three chances to earn one, beginning in the seventh grade. If he hadn't done so by the ninth, he was guaranteed oblivion.

For a boy like Charles Padgett—one who, though he had never missed a day of practice, had only about six minutes of actual game time to his credit (and that at the tail-ends of one rout and two lost causes)—the prospect of that assembly was terrible. He all but knew he wouldn't be getting a sweater, and he simply had to have one.

He had to because he had a girl, Sharon Simpson, whom he loved dearly, who was counting on him. That was the deal: the boys won the sweaters, but the girls wore them.

And that's why, waiting for the light to change that morning, Charles stood on the curb across the street from the campus taking slow, deep breaths and trying not to hyperventilate. He had on his red windbreaker and he kept fiddling with the zipper, taking it up, now down, now up again. When the light turned green, he crossed the street and picked his way through milling clusters of students as he made for the big oak tree, up by the side door, reserved by tradition for the team. The crowd around the tree was even bigger than usual, he saw. All the first-stringers were there. He could see Pinky Bradley and Mule Danforth trading licks. His own arrival was barely acknowledged. One boy nodded, another said, "H'lo, Padgett."

And before he could reply a fist came whistling out of the pack and stopped, quivering, just a fraction of an inch from his nose.

"You flinched, Padgett."

"No, I didn't, Mule. I was just stopping walking."

"Did he flinch, Pinky?" Mule Danforth said.

"He flinched," Pinky Bradley said. Pinky was the team captain; he spoke with authority.

"I was just getting here," Charles insisted. "Maybe I stumbled or something, but I didn't flinch. Honest."

"You flinched, Padgett!" It was a chorus.

And that settled that. Charles turned his right shoulder to the Mule, braced his arm against his ribs, and got ready to pay the price for flinching.

The blow came swift and hard. It caught him on the point of the shoulder and sent him reeling away like a drunk.

"Good lick," said Pinky Bradley.

"Yeah. Nice going, Mule," Charles said. "You prob'ly broke my damn arm." He offered the arm, limp, to Mule Danforth, who took it in his left hand, licked two fingers of his right, and slapped a big moist X high on the nylon sleeve of Charles's windbreaker. It was part of the ritual; if you didn't wipe them off, you could be hit in return.

With that out of the way, the oak tree crowd turned to more pressing matters, and Charles was left to circulate among them in the cautious, shallow-breathed manner of one who knows his credentials are suspect. "You'll have two stripes and a star on yours, huh, Pink?" someone was saying. "Yeah, but I'll have three stripes on mine," said Mule, the team's only three-year letterman. There was no boasting in his tone. It was dry, statistical, a feudal land baron announcing that everything south of the river was his. Nobility felt no need to brag.

The talk stayed on sweaters, what they'd be like and so forth, until it dawned on Charles that despite the freshness of the late fall air all the other boys were in their shirt-sleeves. Stealthily, he unzipped his red jacket, eased it off, and hung it over his shoulder. If only he had a place to bury it.

At 8:20, the first bell rang, and Charles and the others joined the general movement toward the big, three-story brick school building. Inside, walking its corridors, the jangle of book lockers in his ears, Charles realized how much he liked this old building, its sounds and smells. Here, in these classrooms, he more than held his own.

"Charles! Oh, Charles!"

It was Miss Klepke, the principal, calling to him from the doorway of her office.

"Yes, ma'am?"

"May I see you for a moment after this morning's assembly, Charles? We need to discuss your skit for the Christmas assembly."

Charles was the school's performer. He made all the speeches, welcomed all the dignitaries, and, lately, since Miss Klepke had heard his boyish tenor in the First Methodist Church choir, sang all the songs.

"Yes'm," he said. "I'll come by right after it's over."

He got the smile she reserved for him and her other few pets. It was her I-knew-I-could-count-on-you smile. He wished she wouldn't smile at him like that. He turned and walked rapidly away.

Sharon was waiting for him at his locker. He'd been hoping to avoid her this morning. She stood leaning against the corridor wall, her books canted prettily at her chest, a copy of the *Junior Jabber*, hot off the copying machine, peeking from her looseleaf notebook. LETTERMEN'S ASSEMBLY TODAY! screamed the headline.

"Oh, Charles!" Sharon said. "I'm just so excited, Charles! Aren't you? I don't know if I can make it til assembly period or not. Daddy said to me at breakfast, 'Simmer down, Sharon. Just simmer down.' But I said, 'Daddy, I *can't* simmer down—I'm just so ex*cited*!'" She looked at him. "Aren't you excited, Charles?"

"Yeah, I'm pretty excited." He tried to put some excitement behind it. Sharon was an awfully pretty girl, but she was still only an eighth grader. And that was the thing; Charles occasionally let himself admit that the only reason she went with him was that he moved within the aura of the august ninth. Everyone said she'd be a cheerleader next year. She'd get her own sweater then, but until then she was counting on him.

"Daddy says this is one of the most important days in a boy's life, the day he wins his first letter." She searched his face for agreement. "He says it was in *his* life anyway."

Sharon's father was six-four and kept barbells in his garage. When he wasn't selling life insurance, he was usually down at their lake cabin shooting turtles off a log with his .357 magnum. In the months Charles had been seeing Sharon, he'd gotten at most a dozen words out of her father, and six of those had been "Why are you so scrawny, son?" uttered in the frank, uninflected manner of someone who really wanted to know.

"Yeah, well, look, Shar," Charles said now. "I might not get one, you know. Something could happen."

"Charles Padgett! Don't say that!"

He was startled, and a little taken aback, by the genuineness of her shock.

"Well…"

"You'll get one," she declared. "Why shouldn't you? Last year every boy on the team got one." But she was studying him with doubtful eyes now, reappraising eyes.

She was right about last year, though; everyone *had* lettered. And it was this knowledge that had sustained him the past few weeks. If he hadn't come down with appendicitis last August, he probably would have been on that team, and he'd have lettered too. But—and this was the part he tried not to think about—last year they had won the district championship, and this year they hadn't even come close. It was the school board who decided how many sweaters to award, and championships made for generous school boards. But try to explain that to a thirteen-year-old girl who didn't want to hear it in the first place.

"You just have to have confidence, Charles," Sharon was saying. "Daddy says he would never get anywhere in his line of work without confidence. He says losing is the easiest thing in the world, but it takes pluck—and confidence—to be a winner."

"Does your mother ever say anything, Sharon?" Charles said, and regretted it immediately. He mustn't pick on Sharon; he loved her. "Listen," he said, "I've got to get to algebra. I'll meet you back here after assembly, though. Then I've got to go see Miss Klepke about next week's program."

"You going to *sing* again, Charles?" Her voiced flatted on the word sing. They were still trying to forget the assembly last month when Charles, dressed in knee pants, his thin legs exposed to all, had sung "A Little Birdie Told Me That You Loved Me" while holding up a birdcage with a toy canary inside. The song, from a recent Broadway musical, was a favorite of Miss Klepke's. She had pronounced his performance "darling," but the rest of the school's reaction had gone off in another direction. He was still referred to as "Birdie" on occasion, and although it was the closest he'd ever come to a nickname, he could do without it.

"I don't know," he said now. "I guess so, if she asks me to."

"No short pants, Charles. Tell her no short pants."

"No birdcages either, by God."

"Charles! Your language!" He could see she was pleased, though, and he made a mental note.

"Okay," he said. "See you later."

"'Bye, Charles. And remember, confidence!"

In algebra class, he sat on the outside row and stared out the window. A breeze had come up and was whipping leaves and scraps of paper about the campus in little whirling eddies. His eyes went to the big oak tree, the hallowed oak whose black, now almost barren branches, had spread themselves fondly over generations of Mansfield athletes. The wind was picking at its few remaining leaves. Idly, he selected a leaf, a crisp brown one far out on the nearest limb, and told himself that if it was still there when the class ended, he would get a sweater. Almost immediately, the leaf was whisked away. He selected another one.

The angry rapping of a blackboard pointer brought him back inside. "Emil Danforth," the algebra teacher, Mr. Earnhart, was saying, "you and Pinky Bradley will either stop that whispering or leave this classroom. Is that clear?"

"Yes, sir," Mule said, grinning. "We're just real excited and all, Pinky and me. Big day, you know."

"Would it excite you to fail algebra?" Mr. Earnhart said, but he was already on the defensive and bluffing; everyone could see that.

"Oh, no, sir," the Mule and Pinky Bradley said in unison, their big, confident grins drawing admiring titters.

"Well," the teacher said—he too was grinning now; he knew how to lose anyway—"straighten up and fly right then." He returned to his blackboard with relief, and Charles glanced at the wristwatch of the boy across the aisle. Only ten more minutes. It seemed as if he'd just sat down.

Then it was that split instant before the bell rang and everyone was snapping their books shut and swinging their feet into the aisles, getting ready to explode out of there. Mr. Earnhart stopped mid-sentence and placed his pointer in the trough. The bell rang.

Charles was caught up and carried in a tidal surge that took him down the stairs, along the main corridor, and on into the cavernous auditorium. He slipped into his assigned seat and watched the other students spill in through tributary doors on three sides of the huge hall. Onstage, the curtain was already pulled back, and the school band sat in instrument-jiggling readiness. A trumpet blatted experimentally, a tuba whooped. Herschel Mergandahler squeezed in and sat down next to Charles. Fat, asthmatic Herschel always sat by him in assembly. He'd been on the football team too, but with a difference. Herschel didn't give a damn. He only went out because his father insisted. The prospect of not lettering held no terror for him.

Charles decided to make Herschel the index of his chances. If Herschel lettered, so would he. The names would be called alphabetically, and Herschel's would come before his.

They were on their feet now, pledging allegiance to the flag. Then the band commenced a ragged, tromboney version of the "Notre Dame Victory March," with the student body supplying local lyrics ("Cheer, cheer for old Junior High/ Rattle the rafters with the reply…"). When the song ended, Miss Klepke, apparently unwilling to turn so much as her side to her students, slipped crabwise onstage. She smiled blindly and smoothed down her dress, waiting for the crowd noise to subside. Then she glanced offstage, said she supposed this was what they had all been waiting for, introduced Coach Hardy Flowers, and fled.

Coach Flowers bounded out onstage, his weight carried forward on the balls of his crepe-soled shoes, ready to pivot in any direction. He rubbed one big knuckle in his ear, acknowledging—and thus prolonging—the ovation. Then he stood helpless before the student body's adulation for a full minute before asking for a little quiet, please.

Very quickly, he summarized the past season: not a championship year, maybe, but nothing to be ashamed of. Then he moved into the body of his address, using as a sort of topic outline the same maxims that, framed, lined the walls of his office in the basement of the boys' gym. He said a team that wouldn't be beat, couldn't be beat. He said it wasn't the size of the dog in the fight that mattered, it was the size of the fight in the dog. He said when the going got tough, the tough got going. He said his boys didn't know the meaning of the word quit.

"Whether it's the game of football or the game of life," he told them, "the fella who keeps plugging—the fella with the intestinal fortitude—is the fella who's gonna rise to the top. 'Intestinal fortitude': you spell that g-u-t-s, students—" Here he looked toward the wings at Miss Klepke, as he always did when his rhetoric skated onto the thin ice of anatomy, and she gave him her good-sport smile.

"There are lots of parallels between those two games, football and life," he continued. "Irregardless of what field of endeavor you students eventually find yourself entered into— I'm speaking primarily to you boys now—the training you get on the gridiron will see you through."

"When the Duke of Wellington said the Battle of Waterloo was won on the playing fields of Eton, students, he didn't mean that was where they fought it. No, sir. He meant his soldiers whipped Napoleon's because they played a lot of football—and other sports too, I suppose—in school. And I'll tell you this: the Second World War wasn't won by the kind of fella who spent his schooldays sitting around on the seat of his pants."

"You spell that a-s-s," Herschel Mergendahler whispered.

But Charles barely heard him. He was busy with a vision

of green-and-gold sweatered English skirmishers advancing resolutely on a disintegrating rabble of Frenchmen, each of whom looked as if he'd been born knowing how to define quit and hadn't an inkling of how to spell intestinal fortitude.

"So, in conclusion," Coach Flowers said, "just let me say that I'd like to be able to award a sweater to every boy who gave up his afternoons this fall to come out there"—he motioned vaguely in the direction of the practice field—"and helped make the Golden Hornets the fightin'est team in the whole darn state." He paused and looked out over the sea of young faces. "That's what I'd *like* to do, I say—but, of course, that's impossible."

Charles felt a cold wind pass over his heart.

"And so, to all you boys who aren't going to receive a sweater today, just let me say: Thanks, men. It was appreciated." Coach Flowers motioned to the wings. "Okay, bring out the boxes."

A pair of self-conscious seventh graders began pushing and scooting two large cardboard boxes onstage to loud applause. Coach Flowers waited until they departed, then opened the first box and brought out a sweater. He displayed it beside him like a matador. It was made of a shiny, synthetic fabric and dyed a deep, black-based green. It had bright yellow, not gold, piping around the neck and down the front on either side of the buttonholes. There was a left waist pocket, and where the right one might have been was, instead, a large gold block M. It was a beautiful M.

Coach Flowers looked at the nametag inside the pocket and called out the first name: "Willis McClure."

A small boy rose on the far side of the auditorium, pushed up his glasses, and moved toward the stage on a wave of applause. Willis was the student manager; his M would be qualified by a stitched-in "mgr."

Next, the sweaters for the cheerleaders were lifted out, and three girls and three boys went forward to be rewarded. Their M's would bear tiny green megaphones.

An expectant, rustling hush settled on the auditorium. It was time for the real sweaters to be presented. Charles looked to the rear of the room where the eighth graders were seated and found Sharon. She was leaning forward, her hands gripping the back of the seat in front of her, her eyes fixed on those boxes.

"Asapp," Coach Flowers announced. "Roger Asapp." And a large swarthy boy stood up and moved forward to a rattle of applause.

Pinky Bradley was next. He received a huge ovation, augmented with cheers and whistling, as he moved to the stage. The coach shook his hand and gave his shoulder a fatherly squeeze. "My captain, students," he said. "Best little team leader I ever had. Doesn't know *how* to lose."

Then: "Emil—Mule—Danforth." His applause at least equaled Pinky Bradley's. The coach greeted him almost shyly, as if confronting a rare equal. "The big Mule, students," he said. "One of the few three-year lettermen in the history of this school. Let's show Mule what we think of him." And they did, and they did.

After that, though, the list moved rapidly: "Eubanks… Ford…Hargett…Johnson…Jordan…Kroenig…Matlock… Mauldin…" Then it skipped to Nesbitt—no Mergendahler— and Charles felt it in his chest again, though not as cold this time, more like a cool breeze. He glanced at Herschel, and Herschel looked sleepy. When the names jumped from Ortega to Ratcliff, he hardly felt anything at all.

Then they were on their feet again. The band, all clarinets and bell lyres now, was playing "The World Is Waiting for the Sunrise" and six hundred young voices were singing:

> *O Junior High, now hear your sons and daughters*
> *Pledge anew their loyalty to you.*
> *Down through the years our love will know no waning,*
> *Junior High, we sing to you….*

Win a Few, Lose a Few

Up onstage, a beaming, toe-scuffling semicircle of green-and-gold-sweatered lettermen accepted their classmates' adoration.

"Win a few, lose a few, Padgett," Herschel Mergendahler said to Charles on the way out.

Sharon waited at his locker, her whole posture a symphony to shame. Head down, Charles tried to ignore her. He opened his locker, put away his algebra book, and got down the one for civics.

"Charles?" Sharon said. "I just want you to know, Charles, I think it's pretty unfair."

There was just enough ambiguity in this to leave him with no starting point for whatever it was he'd planned to say to her. He studied his feet. "Oh, well," he said finally, "win a few, lose a few, huh?"

"Oh, Charles."

"Yeah, well, listen. I gotta go. I gotta see Miss Klepke."

"All right, Charles, you just run along." There was resignation born of too much suffering in her voice. "But answer me this first. What am I going to tell daddy when he asks me, 'How'd it go today, Sharon?'"

They were both spared his answer by the sudden approach of Pinky Bradley, Mule Danforth, and several other lettermen. They came swinging down the corridor, arms linked, a shouting, shoving phalanx of green and gold. Pinky Bradley pulled the line to a shuddering halt. "Hey, Sharon," he said brightly. "Hey, Padgett. How's it going?"

Sharon flashed him the smile that made her a cinch for cheerleader next year. "Hi, Pinky," she said. "That's a mighty pretty sweater you've got there."

"Thanks," Pinky said. "I'll have to let you wear it sometime."

Swell, Charles thought.

And at that moment, Mule Danforth, bursting with animal spirit and eager to make his presence known, stepped forward, grinning. He dropped his shoulder and brought up a right uppercut that quivered to a halt an inch from Charles's chin.

"Flinched again, Padgett," he said.

It was true. He'd flinched; no doubt about it. Charles didn't even argue this time. Actually, he sort of welcomed the martyrdom. With baleful dignity, he offered his shoulder to Mule to do with as he would. He halfway hoped Mule would knock him through the wall.

But Danforth crossed him up. In a gesture Charles could only interpret as pity, the big letterman placed a gentle, token tap on his tensed right arm, then turned to walk away with the others.

Charles stood motionless for a second, his arm still braced against his side. Then he decided that that token tap simply would not do. It was totally unacceptable to his new mood. "Hey, Danforth!" he shouted to the retreating green backs. "You forgot to wipe it off!"

The lettermen stopped, then shuffled back as a group, with Mule leading the way. Wordlessly, he offered Charles his thick shoulder.

Charles shifted his civics book to his left hand and took a step back to give himself room. He balled his fingers into a knobby fist and, aiming dead center for the three gold stripes on Mule's sleeve, swung with all his might. The smack was satisfyingly loud.

"Ow!" Mule Danforth said. The expression on his face wavered between pain and outrage. "Christamighty, Padgett. What's got into you?"

"Yeah, Padgett," Pinky Bradley said. "What's wrong with you? You being a sorehead?"

A sorehead was not a good thing to be. In the lexicon of Coach Flowers, one of the chief ways the world divided was between soreheads and team players.

"Nothing's got into me," Charles said. "He forgot to wipe it off, so I hit him, that's all. It's part of the game, Team Leader."

"You're a sorehead, Padgett," Pinky Bradley declared.

"Okay, I'm a sorehead."

"You don't have the guts to do it again," Mule said

menacingly, rubbing his arm.

"Maybe I do."

"Maybe you don't."

"Ahhh, come on, Mule," Pinky said. "Leave the sorehead alone."

He began steering the lettermen away. They straggled off slowly now, their ranks broken, and all because of one sorehead. "You just better take it easy, *Birdie*," the Mule shot back over his shoulder.

"Yeah, you too, Mule," Charles said. "All you guys take it easy now, hear?"

He was just pleased enough with his own parting sally to replay it in his mind, which caused him to smile, briefly, as he opened his locker again and took out his red windbreaker. He looked at Sharon, who stood with her books clutched up tight, a stunned look on her face. It seemed like days since he'd seen her.

"I gotta run, Sharon," he said, slipping the windbreaker on. Then, remembering, he added gently, "I don't know what you should tell your daddy, Shar. Just tell him anything you like, I guess."

There was a bit of a bounce in his step—not enough, though, to catch a disinterested eye—as he walked away from her, down the cold, oblivious corridor. He glanced up at the big clock on the wall and saw that he'd have to hurry if he wanted to see Miss Klepke about next week's program because after that he was going to have to swing by the school nurse's office. The knuckles on his right hand were swelling fast, and he had an idea the damn thing might be broken. He hoped it was.

Occurrence at 133 Park Street, Apartment 2A

It all started about a month ago now, soon after Janet moved out. I awoke from a fitful sleep that Sunday morning with an overpowering need to scratch. There was an area several inches above my right knee that was itching like crazy. I had never experienced anything like it. I mean, I've felt the need to scratch before—all of us do—but never anything like this.

So I scratched. And scratched. And scratched. Until gradually the torment began to lessen. Ahh, I thought. At last, some relief. Now I can get out of bed and go fix breakfast. I sat up and swung my feet over the side, but before I could even start feeling for my slippers, this other thing happened. More or less in the epicenter of where I had been scratching, something began pushing its way up through the skin of my thigh. I have somewhat hairy legs—as Janet was wont to remind me—and at first, it wasn't easy to make out what was going on. It looked, through the underbrush, as it were, as if a largish pimple was forming right there before my eyes. One of those time-lapse photography deals, you know, where the growing process is speeded up so the viewer can observe the miracle of nature at work. Pretty weird, I thought. I'm a bit old to be having pimples, but what are you gonna do? As I continued to watch, though, more or less mesmerized by the activity of my own body, what had at first looked like a pimple began, as it continued increasing in size, to take on the appearance of a dome, complete with what I have since learned is called a finial projecting up from its center. *Damn*, I thought to myself. *Would you look at that?*

But I didn't even have time to marvel at what was taking place down there on my leg, because even as the dome (with finial) was emerging, tremendous itching began to occur on the perimeter of this central event. And before I could engage in much more than a preliminary scratching of the affected surfaces, new irruptions began to occur—four of them!—more or less simultaneously, and new objects began pushing their way up through the skin of my thigh. These were not dome-like. They were more on the order of narrow spires: very vertical, very pointed, but with rounded shafts.

So now I had a dome emerging in the middle of my leg and four spires pushing up around it—east, west, north, south—to nail down the corners of whatever was going on. *My God on earth*, I thought. *What is happening to me?*

By now, all thoughts of breakfast, all thoughts of getting up, had vanished from my mind. I intended to sit there on the edge of my bed, on this fine Sunday morning in late June, and watch whatever was happening, happen. I decided to become a spectator at my own transmogrification. So I sat, and I watched as the building beneath the dome emerged, and then the plinth beneath the building, and then the reflecting pool out front, and the formal gardens, and finally the outlying ancillary structures making up the whole of the compound. When it was all over and done with, and no more irruptions seemed to be forthcoming, I simply sat and marveled at what had been wrought on me.

Because here's the thing, reader. It was gorgeous to behold.

I'm not sure now at what point I began to recognize it for what it was. I only know that slowly it began to occur to me that I knew what I was looking at. Mine was an aerial, a bird's-eye view, so to speak, and what I was gazing down on was nothing other than the Taj Mahal! Right there on my leg!

Like most Westerners, I suppose, I was aware of the Taj Mahal as a phenomenon, as an architectural wonder and all that, but I had only a passing familiarity with the particulars of the place. I knew that it had been built by a sultan or maharajah or somesuch for one of his girlfriends, but that was about it. In the days that followed, you may be sure that I read up on the subject. And what I learned was that the Taj was, in fact, a mausoleum, and that, yes, it had been built by a Mughal—which is to say Muslim—emperor named Shah Jahan for his wife, one Mumtaz Mahal, who had died in the effort to present him with their fourteenth child. The emperor loved her so much, I learned, that after she died, in his grief, all his hair fell out. The Taj was a love offering in white marble. A thousand elephants had been used to haul the materials to the building site. And twenty-eight different kinds of precious and semi-precious stone were embedded in the marble to give it its glow. There was jasper, crystal, and jade from China, turquoise from Tibet, lapis lazuli from Afghanistan, sapphire from Sri Lanka, and carnelian from Arabia. Inside the mausoleum, underneath the dome, the tombs of Shah Jahan and Mumtaz Mahal sit side by side, largely unadorned, as is the Muslim custom. Rabindranath Tagore, the Bengali poet, perhaps best summed up the essence of the Taj Mahal. He called it "a teardrop on the cheek of time."

And that, reader, was what I was now carrying around on my right thigh. Because, let's be sure you understand me, *this was not a replica. This was the real thing.* Looking down from the heights, as it were, I could see tour buses pulling up outside the main gate of the complex, disgorging their burden of gawkers. I could see lovers strolling on the walkways beside the reflecting pool, see gardeners trimming the hedges along their route.

All this began a month ago now, as I say, and I haven't left the house since. One reason, of course, is that due to all these extrusions on my right leg I can't get my pants on. But beyond that, and more importantly, they need me here. I have become central to the proper functioning of the compound. I first noticed this several days after the event. I was already aware that the Taj had the ability to change colors according to the available light. That is to say, it might be pinkish in the morning when I first woke up, then milky white in the evening when I went to bed, and sometimes, beneath the light of a full moon, a truly lovely golden hue. But, at first, I didn't connect this with anything I might or might not be doing. Then, one morning after an unusually good night's sleep,—one of the first I'd had, I must tell you, since Janet moved out—I awoke feeling better than I had felt in weeks. I had forgotten all about what I had down there on my leg, and, sitting up in bed, I glanced down, through some low, overhanging clouds, and there, of course, it was: the Taj. I could see workmen sweeping the walkways, getting ready for the new day, see a gardener pruning a hedge beneath one of the minarets, see souvenir salesmen setting up their stands outside the main gate. And the sight of all this, coming as it did as a surprise to me even after all these days of its being there, caused my face to break into a broad satisfied smile. And as my smile broadened, I began to notice that the Taj's color began to change. It went from a pale early morning gray to a pink and then to a beautiful rose-colored hue. And the wider I smiled, the rosier it grew. Amazing, I thought. I seem to be affecting the very quality of life down there. I could see the workmen pausing with their brooms and looking up at me, the gardener leaving off with his shears to do the same. Experimentally, then, I decided to frown for them, and, sure enough, as soon as I began to frown, the rose faded back to pink and then to a sort of lusterless gray. Wow, I thought. That's pretty impressive. I'm having quite an impact down there. That night, I stayed awake until midnight viewing the Taj, gone silent and deserted now, in the murky gloom of my bedroom. At the stroke of midnight, though, I broke into a wide smile and there, down below, sure enough, the entire compound was suddenly bathed in this luminous golden glow. It was absolutely beautiful. The Taj Mahal in full moonlight is a sight no one on earth should have to do without. And with that came, slowly, a realization on my part of the responsibility I now had. It was not a small one. The Taj Mahal had been in existence for going on four hundred years now. It had been offering pleasure and surcease to generation after generation of visitors and pilgrims. And whether or not it would continue to do so was, apparently, in no small measure up to me. I had become its sun and its moon. Its weather and its daily outlook were dependent on me. Quite a responsibility, I hope you will agree.

Still, I didn't feel burdened by the knowledge. Not at all. I felt, in fact, ennobled by it. I had a role now, a part to play in an important, ongoing spectacle. People *needed* me. It gave me a feeling of exaltation, is what it did.

I only wish Janet were here to share it with me.

Happy Birthday, Dear Darrell

There were four of them—two that looked like apple and two that looked like something else—and from where he stood, outside in the rain, PFC Rutledge could almost imagine he could smell them. He watched intently as the cook, a muscular black man in kitchen whites, moved about busily inside, preparing them for the oven. But he waited until the oven door had been opened and the last one shoved in before stepping up onto the back porch of the Camp Napunja Officers' Mess and knocking. The time was shortly before midnight—or 2400 hours, as they like to say in the Marines.

At the sound of the knock, the cook looked up. Then, closing the oven door, he stepped warily over to the back door of the kitchen.

"Who's at?" he said.

"Guard," Rutledge said from outside. He had his cheek

pressed against the glass and he was trying to see in through the steamed-up doorpane as, meanwhile, the rain continued to beat down on his helmet liner and poncho, to run in rivulets down the barrel of his butt-slung M-1.

"What you want, guard?" the cook said from inside.

"Coffee?" Rutledge said. "You got any coffee?"

"Nope," the cook said. "No coffee. Coffee's all gone."

"What's that in that big pot then?" Rutledge said.

"Which big pot?"

"Over by the sinks. The silver one, with the handles. What's in that?"

"Ain't coffee."

"You sure? Can I come in and see?"

"Nossir."

"Why not?"

"'Cause it ain't coffee, that's why," the cook said with some exasperation. "Why would I lie? It *was* coffee, but it ain't now. All it is now is grounds."

Outside, Rutledge fell silent. He still had his cheek pressed against the glass. It was still raining.

"How about a drink of water then?" he said. "Can I have a drink of water?"

The cook laughed. "*Water?* You're out there in the *rain*, man. Drink that."

"Aw, come on," Rutledge said. "Just let me inside for a minute. It's cold out here. My feet are wet."

"Nossir," the cook said again. "No guards in the kitchen. That's the rule. Captain Burlingame'd have my ass."

"Aw, man. Just for a minute. Don't be so hard."

"I ain't being hard. That's the rule, that's all."

"They're all drunk up front anyhow. They'd never know."

"Makes no difference. That's the rule."

"What kind of pies were those?"

"Which pies?"

"Those you just put in the oven. What kind were they?"

"Officers' club kind. That's what kind."

"Looked like apple to me. Apple and something else."

"Is that right? Well, listen up. I can't stand here talking through this door no more. I got work to do. I still got my bread to bake."

"What kind of bread?"

"Man, what difference does it make? None a your damn business what kind."

Rutledge fell silent again. He stood there fiddling with a rubber band he'd slipped around his wrist earlier in the day and then forgotten about until now. The rain, still falling, made a soft, pittering sound on his helmet liner.

"It's my birthday," he said through the door.

"Do what?"

"I said it's my birthday. I'll be nineteen come midnight."

There was a moment of silence on the other side. Then, "Shit, man. What're you trying to do to me?"

"Nothing. It's my birthday, that's all. I felt like telling somebody, and you're the only one around."

There was more silence. Then, "Well, happy birthday, man. Now get your ass off my porch 'fore I call the corporal of the guard."

Goddamn cooks, Rutledge thought, as he stepped down off the porch. Might as well be talking to a rock. Those people were all alike. Wouldn't help you if your life depended on it. Wouldn't even *spit* on you if you were dying of thirst in the desert. He checked his watch. Quarter of twelve and his relief wasn't due until two o'clock. Oh-two-hundred.

He made his way in darkness up toward the front of the officers' club, avoiding the standing water as he went. All the club's windows were shuttered against the rain, so he couldn't see in. But he could tell from the noise level they were having a good time in there. Probably watching another stripper down from Japan. They'd had one last week who could pick a fifty-cent piece off a Coke bottle with her you-know-what. Carmichael had told him about it. He'd *seen* it, he said.

Out front, the rain made haloes around the streetlights. The lights were up on tall poles, and as he stepped out under them, he improved his military bearing, in case anyone was watching. Then, head up, shoulders back, he moved off down the street in the direction of the sickbay and the base library, both of which were dark now, he saw. When he'd come on duty at ten, they were both still open for business, though the sickbay had been in the process of shutting down. Now, even the light in the night duty corpsman's room was off. As he went past the sickbay, he wondered which beds McAvoy and Fairchild were in and if they were asleep already. Probably, he decided.

Rain, rain, rain. When would it ever end? Back in the barracks, all his clothes were mildewed, including his civvies, and there was green stuff growing in his shoes. They had warned him in San Diego. *Okinawa?* they'd said. *Boy, you're gonna hate it. Just wait till the rainy season starts. You'll wish you were dead.*

Well, it had. And he did.

He was moving past the library now, getting ready to turn onto Iwo Boulevard, which was empty in both directions, he saw. Nobody in the street but him. Ahead was the PX, looming up in the darkness like a big barn. It was the biggest building on base, and one of the few that wasn't a Quonset. It had a beer garden out back and a duty-free gift shop upstairs where he'd done his Christmas shopping: some bamboo placemats for his mother and a jade bracelet for Cheryl. That bracelet had cost him a lot of yen. She hadn't given *that* back, he noticed.

The PX was long since closed. As he came abreast of it, he slowed his pace then stopped. Back behind it, beyond the beer garden, was a long, low building housing the officers' handball courts. And behind those, stored for the season under a heavy canvas tarp, were some golf carts. He'd discovered them there earlier, during his first circuit of his post, and had crawled in under the tarp and sat down in one, using his rifle as a tent pole. It had been raining buckets back then but was cozy and dry under the tarp. He'd sat there like that for a good long while, smoking a cigarette and watching it rain.

He decided to do so again.

Leaving the street, he made his way rapidly back to the shadows cast by the handball courts. Then he moved to the rear of the building and turned the corner. There they were, just as he'd left them: five little golf carts all in a row, each with its nose poking out from under the tarp. He studied them briefly, trying to decide, then climbed back under at the same spot as before, second cart from the end. He settled back onto the same little cushioned seat, still nice and dry, using his rifle once again as a tent pole. Outstanding. His own little throne. He removed his helmet liner and sat it on the seat beside him, then dug under his poncho for his Winstons and his Zippo. He lit up, took a deep drag, and exhaled slowly, through his nose. Then, holding his left hand out before him, he gazed at his high school graduation ring. It had an oval red stone with an inset block 'M.' He worried it with his thumb. It was still sticky inside from where the adhesive tape had been. Finally, he let it drop back in his lap and just sat there, warm and dry and a little drowsy, smoking his cigarette and watching the rain play back and forth over the officers' tennis courts across the way.

The package and the letter had arrived together that very afternoon. They were lying on his bunk when he returned from noon chow. He had opened the letter first, and had read it sitting on his bunk there in the deserted barracks, while the others were still at chow:

"Dear Darrell," it said.

"Sorry it took me so long to write, but you know me. I

couldn't find any paper for the longest time. Then Joanne got sick and we all had to take care of her. Little sisters are such a pain! Grrr!! She says to tell you hello, by the way. So HELLO. (That's from Joanne.)

"I baked you some cookies for your birthday, Darrell, but I don't know if they will get there in time or not. Especially after what happened at Christmas. You would think that Congress or somebody would see to it that our boys in the arm service got their packages on time, wouldn't you? I know I would. Anyhow, I hope you like them. The cookies, I mean. If they taste kind of spicey, don't blame me. That's just the cayenne. I had 'help' making them and that's the 'help's' idea of a little joke. I got as much of it out as I could. I just hope they get there in time—but after Christmas you never know. Ooh, that made me so mad!!!

"Darrell, I have something to tell you and I might as well quit beating around the bush. Daddy says I beat around the bush too much. He's always telling me to just say it, Cheryl, say it. So okay, here goes.

"I have met the nicest person, Darrell. You would really like him, I think. He works across the hall from me here at the courthouse. He's the new deputy driver's license inspector. The two of us have been seeing alot of each other lately (not just at work, Darrell) and I have finally decided that things cannot go on like this any longer. It's just not fair to you. So that is why I am giving you back your letterjacket and your ring. I put the ring in with the cookies and I took the jacket over to your mother's house on Sunday. I had it dry-cleaned first and sewed up that hole in the pocket.

"I know this probably comes as a great shock to you, Darrell. It would me too. But you'll get over me. I just know you will. You'll find yourself a nice girl someday and settle down with her and raise a family together and be very happy. And when you do, Darrell, I just hope the two of you are half as happy as Lloyd and I are. Because you deserve it, you really truely do. And I mean that from the bottom of my heart."

That was the end of the letter. It was signed, "Wishing you the best on your birthday, Cheryl."

When he had finished reading it, Rutledge sat there on his bunk for a moment, fingering the edges of the lavender stationery. Then he placed it back in the envelope and slid it under his pillow.

The package was sitting on the bunk beside him. He picked it up and shook it. It sounded loose, like a jigsaw puzzle. He removed the wrapping twine and undid the brown paper. It was a shoebox. "DeLiso Debs," it said on the lid. He lifted the lid, parted some tissue paper.

For a moment, he didn't recognize what he saw. All the shipping and handling they'd been through had reduced the cookies to rubble. There wasn't a piece in the box bigger than his thumbnail. Except for a slight reddish tinge they looked as if they'd once been oatmeal cookies. There were lots of loose raisins.

He chose a crumb and tasted it. *Wow.* It was spicy, all right. She hadn't lied about that.

With his index finger, he began fishing around in the box. He found the ring over in a corner, wrapped in waxed paper and bound up with a rubber band. He undid the rubber band and slipped it around his wrist. Then he removed the ring from the paper. It was sticky to the touch because of all the adhesive tape she'd wrapped it with to make it fit her finger. He slipped it on his own finger and looked at it. Then he held it out away from him and looked at it some more.

Just then, Carmichael came in through the breezeway from the direction of the mess hall. He had a banana in his hand.

"What's that?" he said, pointing it at the shoebox. "A birthday present?"

"Yeah," Rutledge said. He was still admiring the ring. "You want some?" He offered the box to Carmichael, who gazed at its contents.

"Damn," Carmichael said. "Kinda got beat to shit, didn't they? What were they? Cookies?"

"Yeah," Rutledge said. "Oatmeal. Help yourself."

Carmichael selected a fragment and tasted it. Then he selected another and tasted that. "Oatmeal, huh? You sure?"

"Yep."

"What's that hot stuff?"

"Cayenne."

"What's cayenne?"

"I don't know. Something that makes things hot I guess."

"Oh."

Rutledge shook the box at him. "You want some more?"

"Nah, I'll pass," Carmichael said. "Oh, by the way, Sergeant Flores is looking for you. You've got guard duty tonight. McAvoy's in sickbay."

"Guard duty? Why me?"

"I don't know, Rutledge. It's your turn, I guess."

"What about Fairchild?"

"He's in sickbay too."

"What's wrong with him?"

"Fairchild? I don't know. Prob'ly got the clap or something."

"*Guard* duty? Did he say which watch?"

"Yeah. Ten till two."

"Ten till *two*? Did you tell him it was my birthday?"

"No, it slipped my mind. I really don't think it woulda mattered all that much to him, though—do you?"

"*Guard* duty? You *sure*?"

"That's what the man said."

"Well, GODDAMN-SON-OF-A-BITCH—*SHIT*!!!"

"Yeah," Carmichael said. "I know what you mean."

That was earlier.

Now, out back of the handball courts, under the tarp, Rutledge jerked his head up and looked around. Where was he? His neck was stiff, and he had drool in the corner of his mouth. Uh-oh. He'd fallen asleep! He looked at his watch. One-fifteen!

He'd been asleep for more than an hour! He grabbed his helmet liner off the seat and scrambled down out of the cart, dragging his rifle out behind him.

Standing, he adjusted his poncho and looked around again. He sniffed the night air. Something was different. He looked up at the sky. Stars. It had stopped raining! Hallelujah! He re-slung his rifle, barrel up now, and set off quickly in the direction of the tennis courts. As he went, he listened for sounds. He didn't hear any. Good. It meant they weren't out looking for him yet. Maybe he hadn't been missed.

He made a wide swing around the tennis courts, avoiding the big pool of water by the back gate, and turned up toward the junior officers' quarters. A gravel walkway ran there, between the buildings and the parking lot, and he took that, heading once again in the direction of the rear of the officers' club.

So far, so good. He still didn't hear anything. No shouts, no flashlights, no corporal of the guard. That's all he'd need, was to get caught sleeping on guard duty again, like that time in boot camp. Jeez, what a mess that had been. He'd never forget Corporal Richards: *Rutledge, you shithead! You're lucky this ain't wartime. I'd have your ass up before a firing squad!* Those were his exact words. Boy, was Richards pissed....

He was moving past the junior officers' Quonsets now. They were all dark except for one room in the back of the hut on the end. A light was on back there. Somebody couldn't sleep. Rutledge's boots were making a crunching noise on the gravel, so he stepped out into the grass as he went by, giving the non-sleeper a break. Guy was having enough trouble as it was, he figured, without some dumbass guard stomping around outside.

Beyond the last Quonset, an open expanse stretched away on either side of the walkway for a good fifty or sixty yards. Straight ahead was the officers' club. It was dark now too, he saw, except for the kitchen. Light still shone from in there. It flooded out through the windows and lay in bright parallelograms on the night grass.

As he drew near the rear of the building, Rutledge slowed his pace again. And, still some yards away, he stopped and stood eyeing the kitchen. He had already decided he would steer clear of it this time. He had had enough excitement for one night. All he wanted now was to finish his watch, get back to the barracks, and hit the sack. Tomorrow was bound to be a better day.

He stepped off the gravel walk again and began moving quietly out through the grass. He hadn't gone far, though, when suddenly a voice called out.

"Guard? Is that you?"

Rutledge stopped. There was someone there, sitting on the back steps of the officers' club. He could just make out the outline.

"Answer me, guard. Is that you?"

Rutledge weighed his options. He couldn't see who was sitting there—although he had a pretty good idea—and he assumed whoever it was couldn't see him. So, stand his ground? Turn and run? What?

"Is it, guard?"

"Yeah. It's me."

"That's what I thought. Where you been?"

"Nowhere. Walking my post. Why?"

"Walking your post, huh? Come here. Let me get a look at you."

Rutledge stayed put. "Why?"

"Just come here, man. Quit saying why all the time."

Rutledge took a step toward the porch.

"Closer, man. Come closer."

He took another step. He could see now that it was the cook, the one from before, sitting there on the top step of the porch, peering out at him.

"Just as I figured," the cook said. "Bone dry. You been sacked out somewhere, ain't you, guard?"

Rutledge refused to dignify this with an answer.

"Ain't you?"

"No."

"You're lying to me, guard. Look at you. You been sacked out. You ain't been doing your duty as a marine. The Russians coulda come in here and killed us all in our sleep. They coulda stole our equipment, drank our liquor, raped our women—any damn thing they wanted to. While you be sacked out somewhere. Coppin' some Z's. I'll bet you still got sleep in your eyes, don't you? Bend down here and let me see."

Rutledge remained upright.

"I said bend down, let me see."

"Fuck you."

"Said what?"

"I said fuck you, man. If you're looking to run me up, you better have yourself some witnesses, 'cause you're gonna have to prove it."

"Run you up? Who's talking about running anybody up? Prove what?"

"You are. You're accusing me of sleeping on guard duty. That's a court-martial offense. They shoot you for that in wartime."

"Court-martial? Shoot you? Man, don't be talking like that. I'm not accusing you of anything. I'm just raggin' you, that's all. Just killing time in the middle of the night, same as you. So don't be talking no shit about court martials, and shooting people— okay? Ease up. Where you from anyway?"

Rutledge was glaring at the man. "Why'd you want to give me such a hard time then? You did it before too. Wouldn't even let me have a damn drink of water."

"I'm not giving you no hard time. I'm just raggin' you. That's just my way. Anyhow, I was working before. I ain't now. Tell me where you're from."

Rutledge still hesitated. "Texas," he said, finally.

"Whereabouts in Texas?"

"East Texas."

"Whereabouts in East Texas? Place got a name?"

"Moffit."

"Moffit…" the cook said. "Moffit, Texas… Never heard of it. You got a girl back there?"

"Yeah. No, I did have."

"What happen? She drop you for some civilian?"

"Yeah. Some bigshot. Works at the courthouse."

"What kind of bigshot?"

"I don't know. The driver's license guy."

"The 'driver's license guy'? You mean the dude that passes 'em out or the dude that takes 'em up?"

"I don't know. Both, I guess. It's a small town."

"Well, damn, guard, that's too bad. I'm sorry to hear it. When did you find out?"

"This afternoon."

"Just this afternoon? *Damn*, guard. That *is* too bad. And it being your birthday and all too. You must be feeling pretty low."

Rutledge didn't say anything.

"And then you having to walk guard duty outside in the rain," the cook said, "and some raggedy-ass cook not even letting you come in for a cup of coffee. *Damn*. You must be feeling totally fucked over about now, huh, guard? You must be feeling lower than whale shit."

Rutledge still didn't say anything.

"You hear me, guard? You must be feeling lower than whale shit about now—right?"

He still didn't say anything.

"You know where whale shit is, don't you, guard?"

"Yeah. Right. Bottom of the ocean," Rutledge said. "Listen, I can't stand here talking no more. I gotta go. I gotta get back to my post."

"Go? What's your hurry, guard? You and me just getting acquainted."

"Yeah, well, I still gotta go. The guard truck'll be here before long."

"So you're leaving me, huh? Just like that?"

"Yep. Just like that."

"Dropping me like an old shoe."

"Yep."

"Dropping me like your girlfriend dropped you."

"'Fraid so."

"Damn, guard. You're *hard*. You know it? Why you wanta be so hard?"

"It's just my nature, I guess."

"*Hard*," the cook said again. "Hard as my biscuits. Don't you even wanta see what I got for you?"

Rutledge peered at him in the darkness. "Got for me? What do you mean?"

"Come see," the cook said. "It's why I been sitting out here on this wet porch all this time, waiting for you."

Rutledge held back; it might be a trick.

"Come see," the cook said again.

Rutledge took a tentative step toward the porch, then another. And as he did so, the cook reached behind himself and brought up something on a plate. Rutledge looked at it. It was wedge-shaped and lumpy, but even in the dark he could see what it was: a piece of pie—apple, it looked like—with a big scoop of ice cream on top. The ice cream was beginning to run.

"See?" the cook was saying. "See here what I been saving for you?"

Rutledge was still looking. But now he no longer *could* see—at least not very well—because, suddenly, unaccountably, his eyes were filming over.

"For *me*?" he kept saying. "For *me*?"

"For you," the cook assured him. "Happy birthday, Tex. Better eat it up quick, though, 'fore the cream melts."

Everyone Asked About You

It is Christmas Eve. In the cramped front room of a mobile home in East Texas, a man sits reading. On a couch across from him, just a few feet away, an elderly woman, his mother, lies resting beneath an afghan coverlet, watching him. A color television set is on in the room, tuned low to a Christmas program, but neither of them has been paying it any attention. Otherwise, there are no gifts, no wreaths or tree, no signs of the season.

After watching the man read for a moment more, the woman speaks, resuming a conversation that had been allowed to lapse.

"Are you going or not?" she says. She is extremely frail and thin. There is obviously something wrong with her. Her voice is not much more than a whisper.

The man looks up from his book. "Hm?"

"Are you going over there or not?" she repeats. "They invited you."

There is a Christmas Eve party underway in the house next

door. It is a regular, one-story brick house, not a mobile home. Cars and pickups have been pulling in off the highway for the past half hour, parking in the driveway and up in the front yard.

"Oh, mama," the man says, "I don't think so. They can get along fine without me."

The people next door are his mother's friends. He hardly knows them. The woman had come over with a plate of cookies that morning, had mentioned the party, and asked him if he'd like to stop over. But it was just a formality, he could tell. She hadn't really meant it. And anyhow, the book he's reading has gotten interesting. It's Barbara Tuchman's *The March of Folly*.

There is silence in the little room, except for the faint sound of "Rudolph the Red-Nosed Reindeer" coming from the TV. The man continues to look at his mother, but he feels his eyes being drawn back toward the book.

Finally, the mother says, "I think you should. They're probably expecting you."

The man smiles at this. He shakes his head. "You really want me to, don't you?" he says. "You think it's the proper thing to do."

The mother doesn't say anything for a moment, simply lies there on the couch. On a TV tray beside her, within reach, is a small glass half-filled with water. Beside the glass is a large red-and-white capsule.

"I think it'd be nice," she says finally.

The man is feeling the pull of his book again, but he also feels the force of his mother's will. Next door, another car or truck has just arrived, and sounds of laughter and greeting can be heard as the front door is opened to the new guests.

The man closes the book.

"Okay," he says. "Maybe you're right. I guess it wouldn't hurt me to put in an appearance, would it?"

On the couch, the woman smiles.

The man places the book, a paperback, on a stack of other

books beside his chair. He stands up. He has on a pair of shapeless corduroy trousers and an old brown cardigan sweater, the same outfit he has been wearing around the mobile home for several days.

"Can I get you anything first?" he says.

The mother is gazing up at him. He is a tall man and towers over her. "I'm fine," she says. Then after a pause, "I hope you're not planning to go over there like that."

The man looks at himself: at the sweater, the corduroy trousers, the loafers on his feet. "I thought I would—why?"

The mother doesn't say anything, just continues to gaze up at him from the couch.

"What's wrong with this?" the man says. "They're not going to be dressed up over there, mama. You know that."

The mother doesn't say anything.

"You think I ought to change clothes, do you?" he says.

"I think you'd look better," the mother says.

The man goes into the back bedroom of the mobile home, the room he has taken over since he's been there. He doesn't want to go to this party; he knows what it will be like over there. He slides open the door of the closet and unzips the plastic travel bag hanging on the clothes rod. Inside the bag, next to a dark suit, hang two white dress shirts, a gray tweed jacket with matching charcoal slacks, and three ties, all in subdued patterns and colors.

The man removes the jacket and slacks and one of the shirts from the bag and lays them out on the bed. Then he strips off what he is wearing and changes into the fresh clothes. When he's finished, he turns and regards himself in the mirror of the bedroom dresser. Tie or no tie? The hell with it, he decides, he will go whole hog. Choosing the least subdued of the three ties—it is, after all, Christmas Eve, and he is, after all, going to a party—he steps back to the mirror and begins knotting it.

On the wall beside the mirror, as he works, is an assortment of photographs cropped and matted within a single large frame. The pictures, some oval, some rectangular, some round, capture the man at various stages of his life. There are shots of him as a baby, as a toddler, and as a boy of twelve. Also, as a high schooler in his football uniform, as a young Marine, and as a graduate student up in Iowa. There is a large color shot of him posed with his first wife and their three children on the steps of their Minneapolis home, and a smaller one down in the corner showing him standing with his second wife—this one taken just over a year ago now—outside a bakery shop in Paris. All told, there are a dozen pictures. He ignores them as he carefully knots his tie.

With the tie finally fixed to his satisfaction, he goes back out to the living room. His mother is as he left her, the water and the pill still on the tray beside her. He spreads his arms for her inspection.

"You look nice," she says.

He lets himself out the back, kitchen door of the trailer and crosses the small yard to the neighbors' house.

The party inside is just as he had imagined it would be. These are plain people, his mother's neighbors, he a retired railroad worker, she a practicing beautician. The guests are mostly their children and grandchildren. The weather has been unseasonably mild, even for East Texas, and one of the sons is wearing cut-off jeans and a tank top. There is a large tree with lots of presents underneath it. The man doesn't know a soul. His initial awkwardness is never overcome. Attempts are made to include him in a few conversations, but with little success. He has been away from this part of the country too long. Questions about his mother are carefully avoided. Everyone seems to know. He nibbles at a piece of fruitcake, drinks half a cup of eggnog, and leaves as soon as he decently can.

He lets himself back in through the kitchen door of the mobile home. His mother is dozing on the couch. The red-and-white capsule is gone. The television set is still on; Christmas mass is being celebrated in a vaulted cathedral somewhere back east. He has been gone less than an hour.

His mother opens her eyes and sees him standing there, looking down at her. She smiles. While she was dozing, the little green turban she wears to conceal her baldness has slipped and now sits on her head askew.

"How was the party?" she says.

"Fine," he says. "I had a good time. Everyone asked about you."

She closes her eyes again.

"Are you ready to go to bed?" he says.

She nods.

"Would you like another pill first?"

She nods again.

The man returns to the kitchen, takes one of the red-and-white capsules from a bottle on the counter, fills another small glass with water from the tap, and returns to the living room.

He elevates his mother's head and cups it with his hand as she takes her pill. Then he holds the water glass for her as she drinks.

"Ready?" he says when she's done.

She nods and places one thin arm around his shoulder. He lifts her easily—she weighs nothing—and takes her back to the small side bedroom that has become hers. When he first arrived, six weeks earlier, she could still make it back to the bedroom on her own, using just his arm for support. It has only been in the last week or so that he's had to carry her.

As he tucks her in, he hears the sound of a car leaving next door and a shout of "Merry Christmas!" He arranges his mother's hands outside the covers and bends down to kiss her forehead. As he does so, she lifts a hand up off the blanket just enough to touch, and then feel, then stroke, the lapel of his gray tweed jacket.

"You look nice," she says to him as she closes her eyes. "You look nice."

Tall Gal Speaks Out

I am seven feet, two inches tall, and there's not a damn thing I can do about it. Except maybe kill myself. And believe me, I've considered that. As a senior in high school, I was only six, six. "Only." But now I'm twenty-five years old, and I've just kept growing. The doctors we've talked to are puzzled. They speak of excessive hormonal secretions. They cite pituitary irregularities, but they don't really know. And the plain truth is: I am seven feet, two inches tall and still growing. Still growing!

Yes, I played basketball in high school. Let's get that one out of the way early. It would have been hard for me *not* to play, what with all the pressure being put on me. I didn't want to play, but mother said I should give it a try. "You might enjoy it, dear," she said. So I played, but I didn't enjoy it. All those elbows in the kidneys, all that galumphing up and down the court, all that sweat. And you would not believe what goes on in those locker rooms.   And shower stalls. No, I didn't enjoy it at all. Sorry, mother.

I was valedictorian of my class as a senior. I have always been a good student. I like to read, like to learn things, but when you're seven feet, two inches tall, it doesn't make a lot of difference how smart you are, how much you know. The thing people notice about you, first and last, is your height. That's all they pay any attention to. You might say to them, "I really enjoyed that book by Iris Murdoch. She's one of my favorite authors." But you can tell by the look on their face that all they're thinking is, "My God, she's big. Look at the size of her." It's very discouraging. You find yourself holding back, not expressing yourself, even when someone asks. Once, I was at the library here in my hometown, and I was trying to check out some books—poetry, I think it was—Philip Larkin and somebody else. I placed the books on the checkout counter. The woman librarian, a new one, was busy at her computer screen. When she finally turned to me, she started to say, without looking up, "Yes, may I help—?" But then she did look up and the words just sort of died in her mouth. Her eyes rolled back in her head, and she made this gurgling sound in her throat and fell over backward. Blam. Right there behind the counter at the library. They had to get a paramedic in to revive her.

That sort of thing doesn't happen often. But once is enough. To know that you can have that kind of effect on people is disheartening, to say the least. It turns you inward is what it does. You retreat into your shell, and you just want to stay there. Go away, world, you want to say. I won't bother you if you don't bother me.

I had a boyfriend once in the seventh grade. I was already six feet, two at the time, and he was about five, three, five, four. His name was Hubert. He and I used to go to the Saturday matinee movies at the old Parklane Theater before they closed it down. Sometimes we held hands. Once, we were alone in his parents' house, and he asked me if he could sit in my lap. I thought that was a little strange, but I said okay. I was in this big caneback rocker there in his parents' living room. He just crawled up in my lap and put his head on my shoulder, and we sat there like that for a good long time, rocking. Like I say, it was pretty strange. Hubert. I don't know what ever happened to him. I think he joined the Marines. Maybe he took part in Desert Storm.

No man, or boy, has ever made love to me, in case you were wondering. I'm as virginal as the early dawn on the first day of a mountain Spring. Am I happy about it? No. Would I like for someone to "take" me, make mad, passionate love to me? Well, of course I would. I have the same appetites as everyone else, believe it or not. I may look like a freak, but inside I'm breathtakingly normal. Obviously, though, I intimidate men. The size of me does. And intimidation is not good for the male libido, I'm told. In a situation such as that—intimidation, even fear—I can well imagine that it's difficult for them to achieve their erections. Their little members probably just shrivel up and hide. Once, several months ago, I tried to pay a man to do it. This was in New Orleans. I had taken a bus down there for the sole purpose. There was this house, I was told, where men did it to you for a fee. I knocked on some doors, rang some bells, but I never found the house. Maybe when they saw me, they simply denied that that was what they did. Out of fear, you know. So, no, in answer to your unspoken question, no man has ever made love to me. I could tell you were dying to ask.

Ever since the fifth grade—by which time I was already nearly six feet tall—I've been known as "the tall gal." That's how people have referred to me. They think using the word "gal" with "tall" like that somehow lessens the impact, softens the blow. "Gal" is seen as familiar, homey, a way of making me feel that I belong. At least that's the theory, I guess. They think they're being kind. "Here comes the tall gal," they'll say, or, "Being a tall gal, you must have some opinions on such and so." Sometimes I feel like saying to them, what does my being tall have to do with anything? But I don't. I just hold my tongue. Why prolong the agony?

My father is six feet, two, which is supposed to be a nice size for a man, but my mother is a little tiny thing, only five, one. They love me, they assure me, but sometimes I think they wonder how something like this—me, that is—could have happened to them. I'm reminded of that famous Diane Arbus photograph of the "Jewish Giant," and his parents in their Long Island, or wherever it was, home. They're in their living room, and the giant is bending over to keep his head from touching the ceiling, and the poor little parents are looking up at him as if he were Mount Rushmore or something. It's a very sad picture. It never fails to make me cry. You can understand why.

I could have gone away to college—I had the grades—but I decided not to. I decided to stick close to home, where people know me and are used to the sight of me. It's very tiring to try to make yourself innocuous in new surroundings when you're someone as big as me. It's like saying, pay no attention to that battleship moving down the street, even though you know every eye in town is on the battleship. Very tiring.

That's why I took the job in the tollbooth out on the Tri-State Expressway. It's right outside of town, and I can be there in ten minutes. It doesn't pay much, but I don't need much since I live at home. I get to sit down in the booth all day as I work, and in slow periods, I can even read on the job. I've gone through the complete works of Iris Murdoch in the past year—I adore Iris Murdoch— and I'm thinking of tackling *In Search of Lost Time* next. Sometimes the tollbooth customers flirt with me on their way through. Ninety-nine percent of them are strangers on their way to somewhere else, people I'm never going to see again, and occasionally I flirt right back with them. Facially, I'm not that bad looking I've been told, so I just let them think I'm the girl they imagine me to be. You know, five foot, seven, pert little butt, the whole package. As long as I stay seated, I can get away with it. And they can too.

"Where's a good place to eat around here?" they'll say in a typical—not stunningly original—come on. And if I tell them Raymond's Café or the Lakeview Inn, they'll say something like, "What time do you get off? I could meet you there for drinks and a bite, or whatever."

Usually, the "whatever" comes with a little leer.

"Let me think about it," I'll tell them if I like their looks. "Next time you're through here ask me again."

"But I may not be through here again," they'll say.

"Well, that would be too bad then, wouldn't it?" I'll say, smiling.

Usually, that ends it. Mostly they're traveling salesmen, with charts and presentation kits and the like in their backseats, and I never see them again, but last year there was this one boy, he looked to be in his early twenties, who just kept coming back and coming back. His name was Skeeter, he said. Skeeter! He said he lived up in Titusville, about twenty miles north of here. I stalled him and put him off, the way I do the salesmen, but he wouldn't take no for an answer. Finally, what I did was, I went to Costco and bought this cheap ring that looked like an engagement ring, sort of, and the next time Skeeter showed up I flashed it at him.

He got angry. Right there in his car, right beside the tollbooth.

"Well, why didn't you tell me you was engaged?" he said. "You coulda saved us both a lot of trouble."

"I didn't want to hurt you," I said.

"Well, you've hurt me now, haven't you? How does that make you feel?"

"Not good," I said. "I'm sorry."

"Well, you oughta be," he said. "Women like you need to be more careful about how you treat people. I mean it. We ain't all of us as fortunate as you. Good luck with your danged ol' marriage."

And with that, he tossed his two quarters in the bucket and drove off.

Skeeter. Sandy-haired. Had a gap between his front teeth. Kind of scrawny, it looked like from where I was sitting. I've thought about calling him up in Titusville a time or two; he gave me his number, but I've resisted the impulse so far. Where would it get us, after all? We could talk on the phone, I guess, but that would be it. Since then, though, I've been more careful about who I flirt with in the tollbooth. I try to make sure it's a salesman or someone like that. They're tough, salesmen are, thick hides. They have to be. No way you're going to hurt one of them.

"We ain't all of us as fortunate as you."

I can still hear Skeeter saying that, still see the look of hurt and anger on his homely face. I wonder if Skeeter, poor dear Skeeter, is familiar with the concept of irony. Probably not. Iris Murdoch could fill him in.

I get lonely. I know you're not supposed to admit something like that, certainly not to strangers, certainly not out loud,—it's considered bad form, I guess—but it's the truth. I go home to my room at night and mostly I just stay there. I have my books and my TV set and my records, and my parents will look in from time to time, but that's about it. I tried keeping a journal for a while, but I didn't really have anything to put in it. I got tired of writing, and then reading, woe-is-me sentences and that's about all my journal consisted of. Maybe an occasional quote from Iris Murdoch or some other author I've been reading, but mostly just woe is me. Bor-ing.

That's where I am now, in my room. Writing this on my laptop, for Mr. Larrabee's class. He's the instructor in this writing class I'm taking at the local community college. We've had the doorway to my room enlarged. It now goes almost to the ceiling, which is eight feet high. Along the right doorjamb is the record, in pencil marks, of my increasing height, starting from the eighth grade. I have just come back from measuring myself, and guess what? I'm now closer to seven three than seven two. And that's just in six months, which is the last time I had the nerve to check.

I'm going to wrap this up now and go fix myself something to eat. I'm starved. With a physical plant like mine, you have to keep stoking the furnace. I drink lots of milk for my bones. The doctors recommend it. Otherwise, they'll get brittle and break. What I like this time of night is a big glass of milk and some cold fried chicken, maybe a drumstick or two and a breast. I try to keep plenty of cold fried chicken in the fridge. The deli at Morrison's Supermarket is where I buy it. They also have rotisserie chicken, but I like the fried stuff, with lots of crispy, golden brown skin. Whenever they see me coming, someone behind the deli counter—they're all a bunch of jokers down there—is just bound to shout, "Quick! Hide the chicken! Here comes the tall gal."

Second Wives

The rain that had been falling since Kansas City was turning to snow by the time Bates reached Des Moines, and as he swung down off the interstate there at Ames, looking for a place to eat, it had already started to thicken and accumulate, making him wonder what the forecast was for farther north. He had left Fayetteville, Arkansas, that morning in bright sunshine, with the hope of reaching Minneapolis, and home, at a reasonable hour. Now it looked like he might not get there at all.

"The Garden of Earthly Serenity" announced the sign off to the right up ahead on the access road. It loomed there, pleasingly, incongruously, among a host of others—Taco Bell, Burger King, Long John Silver, Kentucky Fried Chicken—he could have predicted he would find. Chinese? he thought. Why not? It sounded good to him suddenly, and as he pulled into the all but empty parking area out front, he was already making selections from a menu in his head.

Inside, a smiling older gentleman came from behind the cashier's counter to lead him to an available table in the dining room. There, he placed water and an actual menu before Bates.

"Waiter come soon," he said and departed silently—just sort of faded away.

Bates looked around the restaurant's interior. It was as vacant as the parking lot. Only two other tables were occupied. At one, a mixed-race couple—black woman, white man—dined in silence. At the other, a May-December pairing—a gray-haired man with an attractive younger woman who looked only slightly too old to be his daughter—was being a bit more lively. Between mouthfuls, the man did most of the talking. The young woman seemed brightly attentive. The man had a vaguely academic air about him, and Bates was reminded that Ames, like Fayetteville, was a university town.

His waiter, tall, fresh-faced, Caucasian, male, arrived to take his order.

"Egg rolls, I think," Bates said. "And how about your chicken *almond ding*."

"Anything to drink?" the young man said, writing on his pad.

"Hot tea. And some lemon if you've got it."

His table was by a window, and after the waiter went away, Bates sat looking out at the deserted parking lot, the steadily falling snow, the haloed streetlights up on their tall poles. He had driven five hundred miles that day, and he still had two hundred more to go if he wanted to make it home, which, right now, considering the weather, he wasn't sure he did. He had a right to be tired, and he was. Find a motel maybe, call it a day? He massaged his temples and closed his weary eyes.

*

The hostility in the room had surprised him. It had caught him off his guard.

Second Wives

He had had dinner the evening before, down in Fayetteville, with Bill and Darlene Henderson, old friends of his from graduate school. He had phoned them from his motel room just to say hello, and that he was passing through, and they had invited him out to share potluck. Bill had come to the motel and picked him up. After dinner, another couple, the Casserlys, also old friends from grad school, had joined them. Both Bill Henderson and Frank Casserly were on the faculty there at the University of Arkansas.

It was over drinks in the Hendersons' living room that the tension—and hostility—had begun to surface. It came mainly at first from the women.

"How's Marcie?" Jennie Casserly had asked, a definite little edge to her voice. "What are she and the children up to these days? Do you still keep in touch?"

Marcie was Bates' first wife; they had been divorced for about six years now.

"Oh, she's fine," he said. "She's teaching school in St. Paul. The kids are fine too. I see them fairly often."

Marcie and Jen Casserly had been close friends. They had been pregnant together, and then young mothers together, and had formed the kind of special bond that comes from living in close proximity in a student-housing ghetto while trying to maintain a household on no money at all. But that was more than twenty years ago.

"Tell us about your new wife," Darlene Henderson said, also with an edge to her voice. Darlene and Marcie had been fairly close too back in those days, though not as close as Jen and Marcie.

"What would you like to know?" Bates said. She wasn't "new" to him, of course, not anymore. They had been married for more than four years now.

"What's her name?" Jen said.

"Ingrid," Bates told her.

"What is she, Swedish?"

"Part Swedish, part German," Bates said. Then, reconsidering, "Well, no, actually, she's American—like the rest of us. Born on a farm in South Dakota."

"What was her maiden name?"

"Wildberg."

"Not Jewish?"

"No, not Jewish."

There was a pause while they all seemed to think about that; then, "How old is she?" Darlene said in that blunt way of hers.

"How old? Let me see…Ingrid's thirty-six now." Bates watched the two women exchange looks. He himself was in his late forties, as was everyone else in the room except Bill Henderson, who had just turned fifty. "She was only thirty-two when I married her, though," he added, a bit maliciously.

"Has she been married before?" Darlene said.

It seemed an odd question to Bates. He looked at Darlene, who had been married to Bill since she was nineteen. "No, never before married," he said, then, seeing the smirk on Darlene's face, as if this confirmed something for her, almost added, *But she did live with a guy out in Denver for a while*—but didn't.

"What does she do?" Jen Casserly said.

"She's a TV reporter, for one of the local stations in the Twin Cities. She covers health care and the environment for them."

"Where'd you meet her?"

"In a bar," he said, and regretted it as soon as the words were out of his mouth.

"A bar?" Frank Casserly said. Frank, like Bill, was a tenured professor now, but unlike Bill he had grown a bit stuffy, it appeared, over the years. He'd also gained about fifty pounds since grad school. Bates could hear him breathing all the way across the room.

"Yes," he admitted. "A bar."

And then, of course, he'd had to explain to them how this had come about: how it had happened when he was still working for the Minnesota Senate and she was covering the legislature for her station, and how the two of them had been introduced by mutual friends in this club behind the capitol where everyone used to go when the night committee hearings ended, and how he had simply called her up one day after that—he and Marcie were long since separated by then—and asked her out. That made it sound somewhat more respectable, he'd hoped, but he couldn't tell from the looks on their faces.

Nobody said anything for a moment. Then Darlene Henderson—good ol' Darlene—had asked, "And what about Marcie? Has she remarried?"

"No," Bates said, and the two women looked at each other again, as if this too confirmed something.

"But she does have a boyfriend," he added lamely.

This was followed by more silence, which began to lengthen.

"Well. Who needs another drink?" Bill Henderson had finally had to say, in an obvious attempt to rescue the situation.

But it hadn't. The five of them had gone on to talk about old times and current arrangements, but there had been a certain coolness in the room throughout the rest of the evening. It had never really lifted. Bates' feelings were hurt. He felt as if he were being punished, and unjustly. He didn't deserve this, he decided. He had just spent six very difficult weeks down in East Texas watching at her bedside as his mother succumbed to cancer, and now he had to put up with something like this at the hands of people he had thought were his friends. He found himself wishing he had never made the initial phone call. Bill Henderson drove him back to his motel. On the way, he tried to make light of what had happened. "The girls" had treated him "a little rough," Bill admitted, but he hoped Bates wasn't too offended by it. It was just their way of showing how much they cared for Marcie.

"Offended?" Bates said. "No, not really. No more than, say, Custer was at Little Big Horn."

*

He thought about all of this now, as the waiter returned with his tea in a little metal pot. The "girls" had been reacting the way women of their generation often did these days. They felt threatened. They felt as if one of their number had been betrayed. Theirs was the immediately pre-pill, pre-women's liberation generation. They were the last to be brought up on a social model that said the woman's place was in the home, and the man's responsibility was to take care of her and their two-point-four children there. And if each fulfilled his role, she had the right to expect that they would, if not live happily ever after, at least grow old and die together. It was a question of "fairness" to them.

"Can I get you anything else?" the young waiter said, setting the tea on the table.

Bates looked up at him. "Mm?"

"Can I get you something else?"

Pulling himself back to the present, Bates surveyed the table. "Lemon? You were going to bring me some lemon?"

"Oh. *Right*," the boy said, slapping his forehead in self-reproach. "I *knew* there was something, dang it. Be right back."

Bates watched him hurry away again. The boy had a lithe, athletic build and moved with a lightness of step that seemed practiced. He reminded Bates a little of his younger son Justin, only this boy was bigger, better muscled. Probably a college student, he concluded. Definitely not a professional waiter.

A moment later, the boy was back with his lemon—sliced, on a saucer—and his order of egg rolls.

"Anything else?" he said, setting the dishes before him.

Bates looked up at him again. "Chopsticks?"

The boy seemed a bit startled by the request. *Chopsticks? In a Chinese restaurant?* Recovering, though, he surveyed the adjoining tables, then stepped over to a nearby place-setting and snatched a pair from there.

"Here you go," he said. "Try these."

"Thanks," Bates said dryly and smiled as the boy retreated again toward the kitchen. Definitely not a waiter.

Word of his mother's illness had come by long-distance telephone a year ago that past February. Bates, an only child, had flown down to Texas for the operation to remove a softball-sized tumor from her stomach and had come on back north once she was out of immediate danger. He had gone back by car in mid-November, though, once it became clear she had only a few weeks to live, and had stayed on at her bedside until the end. Ingrid had joined them for the first two weeks of December, after wrangling time off from her reluctant, ratings-consumed TV station, and had been a whirlwind of energy and good cheer as she bustled around his mother's small apartment, cleaning up, fixing the meals, doing load after load of laundry.

His mother liked Ingrid, just as she had liked Marcie before her. They were no-nonsense types, Ingrid and his mother, able to look bad times square in the eye as well as good ones. His mother had learned her stoicism growing up in the Great Depression and then raising him as a working widow there in East Texas. Ingrid's had come from being the second oldest daughter in a large family on a failing South Dakota wheat farm. She had worked her way through high school as a waitress in an all-night truck stop. In college, she had swept out sorority houses and babysat administrators' brats.

That was what bothered him most about the reactions of his friends, the Hendersons and the Casserlys. They didn't even know Ingrid, had never laid eyes on her. Yet they had felt free to attack her—and through her, him—with sly digs and innuendo. To them, she was simply a member of a despised category—the younger second wife. They had had no real curiosity about who she was as an individual, as a separate and distinct human being. The women saw her as a threat, the men as an object of his own cheap trophy-hunting.

Talk about "fair"—where was the fairness in that?

*

The young waiter arrived with his food and went about laying it out for him. Bates waited until he had departed, then dove in. He was hungry, he realized. His last nourishment—if that was the word for it—had been a Whopper and a diet Pepsi outside Joplin.

As he ate his chicken *almond ding* with his filched chopsticks, his eye was caught by movement out in the parking lot. He looked up to see two late-model cars pull in, park side by side, and begin quickly discharging some seven or eight riders, all of them women, who then hurried off through the snow toward the front of the restaurant. Moments later, they were being ushered into the dining room by the elderly gentleman and seated, with some little commotion, across the way from Bates, at two tables that had already been shoved together, apparently for just that purpose.

The women were high-spirited to the point of being boisterous. They appeared to be mostly in their late twenties or early thirties and had a uniformly professional look about them. There were lots of tailored blue suits and multi-colored scarves. University administrators maybe, Bates guessed, or possibly someone's real-estate sales team.

As he watched, the young waiter who had been serving him came out of the kitchen and approached the tables where the women were. Immediately a chant went up: "Eric! Eric! Eric!" And as the boy drew near, one of the women reached out, pulled him to her side, and gave him a proprietary hug around the hips.

Bates was both shocked and amused. What he was witnessing had obviously taken place a time or two before. There was a relaxed, rehearsed air to it, and everyone, including the young waiter—Eric?—seemed comfortable with his or her role. The women couldn't seem to keep their hands off him, though. As Bates watched, one of them began stuffing what looked like several dollar bills down the front of the boy's tight-fitting jeans.

Second Wives

After the women had ordered a round of pre-meal drinks—white wine mostly, it sounded like—Eric turned and retreated toward the rear of the restaurant. His departure was accompanied by a chorus of "Oohs" and calls of "Look at those buns!" and "Shake it, baby!" And to Bates' considerable surprise, Eric, just before he disappeared through the kitchen door, did precisely that.

Shocked, again, as he was, Bates couldn't help but smile. Ah, life, he thought. He also couldn't help but think of Darlene Henderson and Jen Casserly. How would they react, he wondered, if they were here and had witnessed what he just had? Would they be offended, or would they enter into the spirit of the thing? He tried to imagine the two of them chanting, "Eric! Eric! Eric!" and couldn't do it. There was simply no way; they were from the wrong generation. And that was when he realized that his complaint, his anger, wasn't with the Hendersons and Casserlys at all, but with himself. He hadn't defended Ingrid the way he should have the night before. He had allowed her to be bullied in absentia and hadn't lifted a finger. It had been much too easy for him to view Ingrid, as the others had, from the perspective of his own generation. And from that perspective, she didn't stand a chance. If Ingrid were over at the table with those women right now, she would have been chanting right along with them. Of this, he had no doubt.

He suddenly remembered the day—almost the exact moment—he had decided he would ask Ingrid to marry him. It was nearly five years ago now. They had gone canoeing with another couple on the Saint Croix River, just east of the Twin Cities, and had put in at a state park for a picnic on the riverbank. Afterwards, lying apart from the other couple on the grass, Ingrid had begun telling him about her girlhood on the farm, near Vermillion, how she had been responsible for bringing in the three dairy cows each evening for their milking, and for feeding the family's chickens and pigs, and how she would sometimes sneak away from her chores to go play house at a special place out in the woods where she kept her toy dishes and her dolls. In the course of telling him all this, she had let drop the information that one day out there in the woods she had decided that if she ever found herself in solitary confinement, she would spend the time wisely by learning how to whistle.

Bates' heart had melted on the spot. It was the casual, offhand way she had said it—as if to imply, aren't those the kinds of things everyone thinks about when they're alone in the woods?—that had touched him so. And for days afterward, just the thought of that sturdy, oh-so-practical little farmgirl covering all her bases like that, preparing herself for any eventuality, was enough to bring a lump to his throat.

Now, why hadn't he thought to tell the Hendersons and the Casserlys that story last night?

"Love her?" he could have challenged them. "Marry her? After that, how could I not?"

Eric, emerging from the kitchen with a large tray on which were balanced eight or so glasses of wine, advanced to the women's table again amid more chants of, "Eric! Eric! Eric!" and further ribald horseplay. Bates watched him move around the joined tables, adroitly side-stepping the reaching hands, fending off the suggestive remarks. The guy might not be much of a waiter, he concluded, but he sure knew how to work a room.

The drinks served, Eric, on his way back to the kitchen, stopped off at Bates' table to deliver his check, together with a fortune cookie, on a little plastic dish.

"Was everything okay, sir?" he asked, sliding the dish onto the table at Bates' elbow.

Bates looked up at him. "Fine," he said, though it really hadn't been; his chicken was undercooked, his rice gummy. "Everything's just fine."

"Can I get you a little more tea or something?"

"No, I don't think so," Bates said. "I've had plenty." He smiled reassuringly at the boy. "Those gals over there are really giving you a workout, aren't they?"

The waiter glanced back over his shoulder, then grinned. "Shoot," he said. "That bunch? They're nothing. You ought to see it when the crew from the state bank examiner's office comes in here. Those women'll undress you right where you stand."

Bates laughed. "Doesn't it bother you? Doesn't it get under your skin a little bit?"

"Nah," Eric said. "I'm used to it. This isn't my only job. I moonlight as a male stripper at a club down in Des Moines, and a lot of these women who come in here know me from down there."

Bates nodded, shocked again. *Male strippers? Female bank examiners?* "Are they good tippers?"

"You kidding?" the boy said. "They're putting me through grad school in ag economics."

Bates laughed. "Well, good luck to you," he said. "And, uh, keep on truckin'."

"Yes, sir. I will."

Bates watched the boy walk away to an accompanying wolf whistle from across the room, then he took out his wallet and placed his payment and his own generous tip on the dish with his check. That done, he cracked open his fortune cookie, pulled out the thin slip of paper within, unfolded it, and read, "CULTIVATE ACCEPTANCE; A RESTLESS SPIRIT TORMENTS THE SOUL."

He refolded the little message and placed it in the left breast pocket of his shirt. Then he stood up, took a last sip from his lukewarm tea, and headed for the door. The black-white couple had departed already, he noticed, unremarked by him, but the gray-haired fellow was still holding court for his attentive ingénue, oblivious to the racket nearby. Bates' path was taking him fairly close to the tablesful of boisterous women, and as he came abreast of them, he couldn't resist the impulse to nod and to offer up a little two-fingered salute.

Then, eager now, suddenly, to be back on the road headed north, weather be damned, he hustled on into the foyer and retrieved his parka from a rack where he'd hung it. As he was putting it on, though, he heard the rumblings of a low chant building behind him, and, looking back into the dining room, he saw that, apparently in response to his little salute, the women were all watching him, and the chant was coming from them. Parka on and zippered, he moved toward the door, with the sound from the dining room still building behind him. He wasn't altogether sure what the women were saying—wasn't altogether sure he even wanted to be—but as he stepped out into the snow-filled air it was beginning to sound a lot like:

"Old guy! Old guy! Old guy!"

Incident at Camp Matthews

Everyone was upset with Tinsley. Banks, his squad leader, was upset. Kniess, the right guide, was upset. I was upset. But most particularly, Corporal Richards, our junior drill instructor, was upset.

"Goddammit, Tinsley!" he kept screaming. "Bend, man! Bend!"

"Lock those elbows, Tinsley! Spread those knees!"

"Push, Tinsley! Push! Get your ass down there!"

It was towards the end of our second week at the Camp Matthews Rifle Range, with the beginning of qualifying just a couple of days away. The problem was that Tinsley still could not assume the sitting position. Rather, he could assume it, but he couldn't *maintain* it, which was the important thing.

In firing the M-1 rifle for qualification, there were four mandatory positions: standing, kneeling, sitting, and prone. Prone was the steadiest, standing the shakiest, and sitting the hardest to get into. To assume it, you turned yourself perpendicular to the target, sat down on the ground, spread your upraised knees, and leaned forward between them, resting your elbows on the little crevices of your inner kneecaps. It was a fine, steady position for anyone who could maintain it, second only to prone, but it was uncomfortable for everyone and a real challenge to all but the leanest, most limber of body types.

"You can do it, Tinsley," Kniess, the right guide, said—he who was so tall and so trim. "All you gotta do is put forth a little effort. Of course, it might help if you weren't so fucking fat."

This is what everybody said, including me. "You're too fat, Tinsley. You need to lose some weight."

To which Tinsley would reply that he wasn't fat, he was simply "short-waisted."

"All my family is," he said. "We get it from our mother."

He was from Middletown, Ohio, and hoped to go into law enforcement when he got out. In fact, as he'd told me and anyone else who'd listen, it was his reason for joining the Marines in the first place. The training and that "USMC" credential on his resume were to be his tickets to a good-paying job with the Ohio Highway Patrol.

But first, he had to master the sitting position.

"What are we gonna do about Tinsley?" all the other recruits, myself included, were beginning to say in our pyramid tents each evening as the day for qualifying approached. "He's gonna bring down the whole unit."

"He's gonna ruin it for everybody."

"He's gonna keep us from making Honor Platoon."

Because that was the thing. You competed at the rifle range, as you did everywhere else in boot camp, against the other platoons in your training cycle. And because every marine is "first and foremost a rifleman," marksmanship scores counted heavily in the final summing up. The minimum qualifying score was 190 out of 250, with failure to qualify an absolute disgrace. And sitting was a mandatory position, worth a total of 50 points.

"Bend, Tinsley!" Corporal Richards shouted. "Spread those knees and *bend*! Goddammit, boy, you're not even trying!"

Richards had been a rifle instructor before he went off to DI school, and though only our junior DI, he was in charge of us on the firing line and responsible for our performance there. I admired Corporal Richards. He was from Tyler, Texas, not far from my own hometown, and had been a fire-team leader in Korea, at the Chosin Reservoir, before his position was overrun by "about a million fucking Chinese." His descriptions during those first weeks of boot camp of the retreat from the "Frozen Chosin"—in which the surrounded marines had brought out all of their equipment, and all of their wounded, and all of their dead—had brought tears to my eighteen-year-old eyes. I was an impressionable teenager, and the story set an example of courage and camaraderie under fire that I hoped to have a chance to emulate some day.

"Tinsley! What are you doing down there, Tinsley? You look like a monkey fucking a football!"

"Spread those knees apart, Tinsley! Lock those elbows! Bend! Bend! Bend!"

It was the last day of practice firing. On Friday, at oh-eight-hundred, the real thing would begin. Corporal Richards had spent more time with Tinsley than with anyone else in the platoon. He had wheedled, cajoled, threatened, implored—you name it. He'd used up his entire DI repertoire on Tinsley and to no avail. Tinsley still couldn't hold the sitting position long enough to get off ten rounds of ammunition with any degree of accuracy. After each round of firing, the waving from down at the butts of the red flag known as "Maggie's drawers" would tell us that, once again, he hadn't even hit the target. As we in the platoon looked on, it grew increasingly clear that Corporal Richards' patience had run out. You could see it in the slump of his shoulders as he regarded Tinsley doing his inadequate, fat man's best down there in the dirt and dust of the firing line, in the way he rubbed his mouth with the back of his hand, then, removing his utility cover, ran the hand up through his lank blond hair.

When it happened, though, it happened very quickly. So quickly I wasn't entirely sure I'd seen what I had seen.

One minute, Richards was leaning over Tinsley, seeming to offer instruction, and the next, he'd taken several steps back from him and was gazing down range at the target area, apparently lost in thought. Then, suddenly, after glancing both left and right along the busy firing line, he pulled himself up like a runner taking his mark, executed a rapid little running jump step, and landed with both heavy field boots squarely between Tinsley's shoulder blades.

I could hear the "*crack!*" from where I stood. It was sharper and louder even than the rifle fire all around us.

And now there was poor Tinsley rolling around, *writhing*, in the dust.

"Somebody get a corpsman up here," Richards said calmly, as if he'd just happened onto the scene. "We've got an injured man."

Tinsley was given a medical discharge. They took him by ambulance straight from the firing line down to the big naval hospital in San Diego, some thirty miles away, and he was gone, out of the Marines, almost by the time we got back from the rifle range. We never saw him again. The scuttlebutt, though, was that he'd suffered not just one, but two broken collarbones as a result of what Corporal Richards had done.

Our platoon still didn't make Honor Platoon, the one billeted right next to us did, but our rifle scores were a whole lot better than they would have been if Tinsley had remained with us, and for that, we were, for the most part, grateful.

Not that there weren't a few dissenters.

"Yeah, but did you *see* it?" they'd say in an outraged voice once we were back at the Marine Corps Recruit Depot in San Diego. "Did you see what Richards did?"

And even those of us who hadn't, who only knew what they had been told, would have to admit that it was a cruel and vicious thing to have done. Uncalled for, certainly. There was no getting around that.

"Answer me this, though," someone would always shoot back, however. "Would you want Tinsley in your fire team? Would you want him protecting your flank when the Chinks came over the hill?"

And everyone would quickly agree that they wouldn't,— "No, sir; no way"—that in the event of another shooting war, as unlikely as that might have seemed in that peaceful, long-ago springtime of 1958, it would be just as well if Tinsley weren't around.

Samaritan (A 70's Story)

The bottle was on the counter in the kitchen, lying on its side.

"Think now," Bates said. "How many?"

The woman, Jocelyn, was standing just behind him in her robe, hugging herself as if for warmth. "I don't know," she said. "I can't remember."

Bates turned to her. "Well, *think*, Joss. Was it half full?"

"It could've been."

"A third full?"

"Possibly."

She didn't seem much interested. She picked at something, an egg stain, on the sleeve of her robe. "Would you like some coffee?" she said. "There's liquor in the cabinet."

It was a Sunday evening, late. The call had come fifteen or twenty minutes earlier, just as Bates and his wife were preparing for bed. He had gotten there as quickly as he could, racing across town in a pounding rain, his sense of urgency only slightly diminished by his knowledge that this was—what?—the third such episode that fall. The previous two times, she had summoned other male members of the department. He knew this because they had told him so.

He took her by the shoulders now. "Look at me, Joss," he said.

She looked at him.

The whites of her eyes were reddened, and her pupils were enlarged, or so it seemed. It was hard to tell, actually. How big were pupils supposed to be?

"How do you feel?" he said.

"Right this minute?"

"Yes. How do you feel?"

"Rotten. Absolutely, positively rotten."

He considered. "Well, what do you think? Should we take you somewhere? The campus clinic? Urgent Care?"

"No," she said. "I've been feeling rotten for weeks. Let's just have some coffee."

Seated in the living room, coffee mug in hand, Bates, breaking a silence, said, "What do you hear, Joss? Anything?"

"Hear? Oh, not much. The boys got a postcard."

"Where, ah, are they now?"

"Mexico."

"Still?"

"That's what the postmark said."

She was on the sofa, across from him. Bates was in a chair. "Have you thought about what you're going to do?" he said.

"Do? What can I do? Go home to mother? I'm thirty-eight years old."

He felt bad for her. It was a terrible thing. "Poor Joss," he said. "How long has it been now? Three months? Four?"

"It's been exactly three months, fifteen days, and, let's see, five hours since he called me from his 'symposium' down in

Fresno. If I had a watch, I could probably tell you the minutes."

"Poor Joss."

"His 'symposium' that he and Little Miss Hot Pants were attending, by the way, on a faculty development grant."

"Is that right?" Bates said, honestly surprised. "I didn't know that."

"Yes. I'm thinking of writing a letter to the editor of the local paper about it. I'm sure the taxpayers of this state would like to know how some of their money is being spent."

"Don't do that, Joss. You don't want to do that. They already think we're a bunch of Communists anyway."

"Well, I might."

They fell silent again, sipping their coffee. There was a fire going in the fireplace, and Bates stared at that. As he did so, a log shifted, sending up sparks.

"The hell with this," the woman, Joss, said. "I'm fixing myself a drink. You want one?"

He looked at her. "Do you really think you should, on top of all those—?"

"I don't know whether I should or not, but I'm going to. You want one?"

"Well, but do you think it's a good idea?"

"I don't *care* if it's a good idea. I'm fixing myself a drink. Do you want one?"

Bates said a small one, and she went out to the kitchen to make their drinks. While she was gone, he wondered if maybe he should call his wife, tell her how things were going. He pondered the etiquette of the matter. How much longer should he stay? When could he decently leave? For situations such as this, what did Emily Post recommend?

Joss returned with the drinks, handing him his. Then she touched glasses with him.

"Cheers," she said. "Here's to love and marriage."

Bates smiled wryly for her. "Here's to *you*, Joss," he said.

"You've been through a heckuva lot. And all in all, you've handled it pretty well."

"Yes, haven't I though? So far, I've only tried to kill myself half a dozen times."

"Come on, Joss."

"At least I haven't burned the house down—right?"

"Come on, Joss."

"Or shot the kids."

"Come on now."

They lapsed back into silence. Bates went back to staring at the fire.

"I've been writing some poems," Joss said. "Would you like to hear them?"

Poems. What could he say?

"Sure, Joss. Let's hear 'em."

She went to a breakfront there in the living room and came back with a loose-leaf notebook. Seated again on the sofa, she opened the notebook up and began reading to him from it. The poems were mostly quite short. Words such as "darkness," "solitude," and "sorrow" recurred often. One poem was called "Despair at Dawn."

"They're…nice, Joss," Bates said when she was finished. "Touching. Powerful."

"Do you honestly think so?" she said. "Or are you just saying that?"

"No, no," Bates assured her. "I mean it. They have a lot of feeling."

"Well, good. I'm glad you like them. It was either write poetry or drink myself to death." She smiled. "So I compromised, and did a little of both." She set the notebook aside. "Speaking of which—are you ready for another one?"

Drink, she meant. Bates looked at his watch. It was quite late. "I don't think so, Joss. If you're feeling better, I probably ought to run. I've got an eight o'clock in the morning."

"Please?" she said. "Just one more? I'm not sure I want to be alone just yet."

"Where are the boys?"

"Upstairs. Asleep. But you know what I mean."

Bates looked at her. Her eyes implored him. He could see the pain. What might she do if he left?

"One more," he said. "Then I've really got to go."

She was away longer this time, and when she came back, she'd fixed her face. Also, he thought he smelled perfume. After she handed him his drink, she went over and stood by the fireplace. Posing?

A moment passed. Then, "Ted?" she said. "Will you answer me a question?"

"Sure, Joss. Shoot. What is it?"

"Look at me."

He looked at her.

"Do you find me…attractive?"

Uh-oh, he thought. Here it comes. Hynes and Brinkman had warned him. "Of course, Joss. What kind of question is that? You're a damn fine-looking woman. You know that."

"A damn fine-looking woman who's pushing forty."

"Well, what the hell, Joss. What the hell. We're all pushing something. The only way to avoid getting old is to die young."

"Ted, the philosopher."

He smiled. "Right. Ted, the Friend of Man."

"And Woman too, Ted?"

"And Woman too."

"But all you men like younger women, don't you?"

"Not really. Not all of us."

"Most of you. You like those tight little butts, don't you? You like those bouncy little tits."

"Come on, Joss."

"Don't you?"

She was glaring at him. Bates didn't say anything. Things were getting tricky, as he'd been warned they might. As he was thinking this, she left the fireplace and came over and knelt down on the rug at his feet.

"Can I ask a favor of you, Ted?" she said.

"What's that, Joss?"

"Would you kiss me?"

"Oh, now, Joss, I don't think we ought to get into anything like that—do you?"

She lifted her face to him. "Please?"

Tricky, tricky, tricky. He bent forward and pecked her on the lips.

"You can do better than that."

He kissed her again, with a shade more feeling.

"Would you make love to me, Ted?" she said. "Right here? On the couch?"

"Come on, Joss. You don't want to do this. You really don't. Think how you'll feel in the morning."

"I'm not worried about how I'll feel in the morning. I'm worried about how I feel right now. And right now I need someone to make love to me. I need someone to prove to me I'm still a woman."

"Come on, Joss—"

"I need that, Ted. I need it very much."

He was beginning to feel hemmed in. They'd told him it might come to this. They'd warned him.

"Don't make me beg you, Ted."

He looked down into Jocelyn Whitehead's upturned face, her pained, imploring eyes. It was a face almost as familiar to him as his own wife's. They had known each other for years. They were good friends. They had danced together at parties, been volleyball teammates at departmental picnics, taken the same side in most of the political arguments of the day. She and his wife were members of the same book club, had led together the local fight to save the seals. Their kids had attended the same Montessori school, for God's sake. But none of that was helping him now, was it?

"Did you hear me, Ted? Don't make me beg."

It was after midnight when he got home. His wife was asleep in their bedroom with her reading light on, a lending-library copy of *Our Bodies, Ourselves*—next up at the book club?—spread open across her chest. He undressed quietly and slipped into bed beside her, trying not to wake her up. As he reached across to switch off her light, however, she opened her eyes and looked at him.

"Ted?" she said. "What time is it? Where were you?"

He reminded her.

"Oh," she said. "I tried to wait up, but you were gone so long I must have dozed off."

He didn't say anything, adjusted his pillow instead.

"How was she?" his wife said.

"Beg pardon?"

"Joss. How was she?"

He considered the question and all its possible answers. It was not, he decided, something he cared to get into. Pillow plumped, covers arranged, he turned on his side and put his back to his wife.

"She'll live," he said. "Please turn off the light."

Osama Fathered My Child

By Melanie G. (as told to the author)

The Middle East wasn't even my idea. I wanted to go to Cancun. But Cindy Sederstrom knew this guy in Chicago who books Holy Land trips for church groups, and he had some cheap tickets due to a cancellation, so almost before you know it we're on a plane to Amman, Jordan—which up to that point, I confess, I'd never even heard of.

How we got from there to Sana'a, Yemen, I'm still not sure. I remember a long train ride and a midnight ferryboat and a convoy of Land Rovers and the sun coming up over these huge sand dunes and then, *Voila!* Sana'a! What a dump. There was a grand total of maybe one restaurant in the whole damn town.

Khalil, Cindy's friend from pharmacy school who met us in Amman and got us down to Sana'a (and kept us supplied with ungodly amounts of *kif* along the way), insisted the town wasn't so bad once you got used to it, but I don't know. He grew up there. All I can say is, it wasn't Gay Paree.

Anyhow, our second night there we went to a party in this high-rise. Up on the top floor, sort of a party room, looking out over the "city," there were about two dozen guys there and, like, maybe eight girls. Great odds, huh? About half the guys had been to school in the States and considered themselves pretty cool. They knew Michael Jackson, Madonna, the Green Bay Packers, stuff like that. Some of them shucked their jellabas at the door and had on jeans and t-shirts underneath. Three of the girls were these blonde missionaries from Provo, Utah. Boy, were they ever out of pocket! They didn't dance, they didn't smoke; I don't even think they *peed*, to tell you the truth.

About midway through the evening, another group of guys shows up and among them is this extremely tall one. I didn't see him come in, but suddenly, he's there, and he's leaning against the wall with his arms folded, and he's eyeing me. Me! Little Miss Two Chins from Waukegan, Illinois! Now, all these guys are rich. They've all got money coming out their ears, but this tall one, everyone says, is really loaded. I mean *beaucoup* bucks. They all defer to him, cut him huge amounts of slack, and he just keeps eyeing *me*.

"Who's the tall one?" I finally ask Cindy.

"Member of the Bin Laden family, Khalil says," she tells me. "They're big in construction and real estate development, here in Yemen and all over the Middle East."

"What's he do?"

"When he's not partying? Studies engineering," Khalil says.

And right about then, Stretch, as I've begun of think of him, detaches himself from the wall, strides over to us, and proceeds to ask me to dance!

The music is mostly old Stones and Led Zeppelin albums, some Doors and some Beatles. Oldies but goodies. Stretch has still got his sheet on, but he hitches it up around his elbows and off we go. He starts doing this sort of funky chicken thing to "Twist and Shout," and it's all I can do to keep from busting out laughing. I mean, he's so tall and so skinny and all, and he's got these arms and legs flying every which way. He's like a scarecrow, with rickets. And he never cracks a smile. Just *serious*. So *serious*. Like this is this Western thing and he's determined to master it. My heart kinda went out to him. I admit it.

Now it's a few minutes later, and we're slow dancing to "Eleanor Rigby," and he's holding me and I'm looking up into those big, wet eyes of his. Wow. You've seen the pictures, the videotapes on CNN and whatnot. Well, let me tell you, they're nothing, *nothing*, compared to the impact of those eyes up close. You thought Omar Sharif had sexy eyes? You oughta try this guy on for size. Mercy! By the time I get back over to Cindy, my knees are shaking, and my mouth is dry as a sock.

"You all right?" Cin says.

"I'm fine," I say. "I just need to sit down a minute."

I don't remember much else about the party, but shortly before things broke up, this flunky dude comes over to us and tells me softly that his boss, Stretch, will pick me up at our hotel in an hour. I'm to go back there and "freshen up." The way he says it it's almost like an order, like I don't have any say in the matter. And for some strange reason, that's just fine with me!

Sure enough, an hour later, this big white Mercedes-Benz pulls up out front of our ratty little hotel and I tell Cindy—who just winks at me; she's got this thing going with Khalil by now—that I'll be back in a little while. "Freshened up," I go down and get in the back seat of the car with Stretch, who's changed into some fresh new duds himself, and we head out of town, a driver up front driving us, to this secluded spot some distance away, overlooking the Red Sea.

When we get there, the driver gets out and wanders down to the beach. Stretch, no doubt remembering how my knees went watery back at the party, puts some Beatles on the tape deck and pretty soon we're dancing to "Eleanor Rigby" again in the sand outside the car. And he's crooning the words in my ear!

Ooooh look at all the lonely pipples
Where do they all come from?

Turns out he's a big fan of the "Biddles."

"Too bad about John," he says to me. "New York must be a very dangerous place."

He's also got liquor and hash, and God knows what all in this little cabinet in the backseat of the car and he urges me to have whatever I like, though he's not drinking or smoking anymore because he's recently got religion, he says. He's getting ready to go to Afghanistan or somewhere. I pour myself a little Johnny Walker and settle back to watch the moonlight play on the water down below. It's pretty romantic where we are. The Red Sea is fairly narrow along there, and you can see all the way over to Africa: tiny lights winking far off in the dark. Also, there's a nice breeze coming up from the water.

Stretch settles in beside me, sipping tea from a thermos cup, and starts making small talk. How am I liking my visit to his part of the world? Are my accommodations at the hotel satisfactory? How big is my hometown? How far is it from Washington, D.C.? What's my favorite color? Do I like the Biddles as much as he does? How often do I fly? Can anyone rent cars in America, or do you have to be a citizen? On and on, one question after another. Who's my favorite movie star? How many toilets on a Boeing 747? At one point, he started talking about architecture. He said he greatly admired "Fallingwater"—which is apparently this building somewhere by Frank Lloyd Wright—but that, structurally, it was unsound. "It will collapse of its own weight one day," he assured me. "Wait and see." I didn't know what the hell he was talking about, to tell you the truth, so I wasn't going to argue with him. I notice that he's squinting as he looks down at me, though, and I realize he's near-sighted! Too bad, I think, glasses or contacts would be a shame for those eyes. But right about then, almost before I know it, he's got his hand down the front of my blouse. I knew what *that* was about. Apparently, *that* wasn't against his religion.

"Whoa, Buster!" I say. "Not so fast." But he just turns those eyes on me, cranks up the wattage, you know, near-sighted or not, and pretty soon I'm silly putty again. And after that, well, the rest is history, as they say.

Now, people have asked me what kind of lover he was, and my answer has always been that it's none of their damn business. I'll just say this, though, for the record: I've had worse. Are you listening, Frank Maldonado?

They've also asked me if he expressed any anti-American sentiments of any kind while we were together. Well, no, he wouldn't, would he? Not while he was trying to make it with an American citizen. *Duh.* Besides, it was just that one night. He promised I'd be hearing from him afterward, but I never did. (Unless you want to count, as some of my cynical friends do, nine-eleven.)

I was already back in school in the States before I realized I was pregnant. Talk about a shocker! I still don't know how it happened. Eli Lilly, you owe me. We considered an abortion, mother and I, but I'd already had one of those when I was sixteen, and I didn't want to go through that again. And, besides, I kept thinking about those eyes, and wouldn't it be nice to have something like those in the family?

So anyhow, that's how little Lance made it into this world. A decision I don't regret for a minute. Not for a minute. You can criticize me all you want. He was born at Sacred Heart Hospital in Evanston, Illinois, on January 25, 1984. He weighed seven pounds, six ounces, and was delivered by Caesarean section. Criticize me for that too if you want to. I raised him as a single parent—though, believe me, at times it wasn't easy—and these days I just couldn't be prouder of him. He's turned into a fine, strapping young man. *Tall.* Big through the shoulders. He wears a size thirteen shoe. You'll say, well, that's just a mother talking, but so what? It's how I feel. I wasn't too crazy about him up and joining the Navy like he did, but what was I going to do? You know how they are at that age. You can talk yourself blue in the face, and it won't make a lick of difference. Trust me.

"Mom," he says, "it's what I want to do. Carl Auerbach is going in, and so is Mickey Templeton. I can go to college afterward."

And that's how it happened. He was out the door before I knew it. I've had just a handful of letters from him ever since. He went through a lot of special training, I know, before heading overseas. He's with this Navy SEALs unit—they're sort of underwater demolition guys, and I don't know what all— and he really seems to like it. He's already talking about maybe re-upping, making a career of it. He was at Bagram Air Base near Kandahar for a while, but they've recently been redeployed to what the papers are calling "the tribal regions" along the Afghan-Pakistan border. It's very mountainous there, rugged, full of caves and such. They'll be moving around a lot, though, on "choppers" and whatnot, going wherever they're needed.

"Well, if you run into your father," I said to him before he left the States—we've always been candid with him on that score, and why not?—"just tell him that fuschia is still my favorite color."

I hope they do meet up. It might make for an interesting confrontation. They're twenty/twenty through a sniper scope, he tells me, no near-sightedness there, but still and all, he has his father's eyes.

Hooray for Hollywood

Butters had been so *lonely*. All his buddies—the guys he'd served on Okinawa with, his boot camp pals, even most of the old Twentynine Palms crowd—were gone now, discharged, and he was still stuck out there in the desert with nearly a year left to do. His new barracks mates were just kids too, teenagers. Some of them had never even *heard* of a four-year enlistment. They considered him part fossil, part fool. And most days, as he moped around the battalion area, rarely smiling, speaking to hardly anyone, that was just about how he felt.

So when the notice appeared on the bulletin board saying one of the Los Angeles TV stations was looking for "uniformed Marines" to fill out its audience for an afternoon talk show, Butters signed up. Why the hell not? It would mean a free bus ride into LA, and maybe a free meal or two, and, besides, what else did he have to do?

About forty of them made the trip. They'd been instructed to wear their dress greens, Ike jackets optional, and when they arrived at the studio, which was in Hollywood, in the old NBC Building off Vine Street, they were seated about midway up on the main level of the small studio auditorium. The rest of the audience, all around them, were women, middle-aged and older. Butters' seat was right on the aisle.

The show was called *Reach Out, LA,* and that day's installment featured a panel discussion on, as near as Butters could tell (his mind kept wandering), "community values." Just before it went on the air, a man in an orange studio blazer had approached him and asked if he'd mind asking the participants a question. Butters said he wouldn't mind, and the man had given him a slip of paper with the question written on it. Butters read it over a few times, memorizing it, then folded the paper into a tight little square and sat holding it in his fist.

About twenty minutes into the show, the "host," or "moderator," or whatever he was, looked out into the audience and feigned surprise at finding Butters and his group seated there.

"*Well!*" he boomed. "*I see we have a contingent from the U.S. Marines in attendance today!*"

Bright lights came on and cameras swung in Butters' group's direction.

"*Marvin,*" the host said from up onstage, "*you want to introduce these fellas to the folks at home?*"

The cameras shifted slightly to Butters' left, and the man in the orange blazer stepped into the lights and spoke into a hand mike. "*Right you are, Doug! These are the men of the First 75's Anti-Aircraft Artillery Battalion stationed out at Twentynine Palms!*"

"*Well, welcome aboard, men!*" the host roared. "*Audience, let's give these guys a hand!*"

There was a round of applause from the women in the audience and from the panelists up onstage.

Hooray for Hollywood

"Marv," the host said, *"perhaps one of these men has a question for our panel."*

"Let's just see if they do, Doug," the man in the orange blazer said, stepping toward Butters. *"Excuse me, corporal. Could I get you to stand up and give us your name?"*

Butters stood up. *"Corporal Donald J. Butters,"* he said into the microphone the man held up for him. *"USMC."*

"Well, Corporal Butters," the orange-blazer man said, reclaiming the mike, *"do you have a question for our panel?"*

Butters bent to the microphone again. *"Yeah,"* he said. *"I've got a question."*

"Go ahead and ask it, corporal," the blazer man said.

Butters recited the question the man had given him: *"'Don't you think it's about time someone started paying a little attention to how the man of the house feels?'"*

There was a titter in the audience and a slight flurry among the panelists onstage, and everyone quickly agreed that, yes indeed, attention should be paid to the man of the house's feelings. Then the discussion moved on to something else, the lights and the microphone went away, and Butters sat back down. Feels about what? he wondered idly. He hadn't been following very closely what was going on onstage before he asked his question (something about how much responsibility do we have, as Christians and members of other faiths, to the strangers among us and to "those unlike ourselves"?) and he didn't follow it very closely afterwards. Mainly, like the others in his group, he was just waiting for the stupid show to be over with—waiting to be released back out into the hot, bright sunlight of pre-Easter Hollywood.

Which, a short time later, he was.

And now it was late afternoon and, for March, still quite warm. Butters had removed the blouse to his dress greens and thrown it over his shoulder, and as he walked along Hollywood

Boulevard, he also loosened his tie and unbuttoned his collar. This put him out of uniform, he knew, but he didn't give a damn. As long as there were no MPs around.

He was headed for the USO. It had been nearly three hours since the end of the television show he'd been on—him! on TV!—and he'd been killing time in typical fashion—a beer here, a beer there, some window-shopping, some sight-seeing, a double cheeseburger and fries—ever since. He'd been thinking too, off and on, about a girl he'd met once, months before, and he'd just worked up the nerve to go call her. That was why the trip to the USO: the phones there ("For Local Calls Only, Please") were free.

The girl's name was Phyllis Beardsley. She lived in Inglewood. He'd met her through a boot camp buddy of his who'd gone to high school with her up in Fresno. She wasn't real pretty or anything, she was just a girl—but, hey, beggars couldn't be choosy, could they?

"Hello?"

"Hello. Is this, um, Phyllis?"

"Yes, speaking. Who's this, please? Who's calling?"

"Well, um, it's Don Butters. You may not remember me. I was with Bud Andress that time—over at Valerie Allen's apartment. In Glendale. I'm a friend of Bud's."

There was a moment of silence on the other end. "The marine?"

"Yeah, right, the marine," Butters said, glad to be remembered.

"From Texas."

"Right. From Texas."

There was more silence at the other end. Then, "So, what can I do for you?"

"Me? Nothing, nothing at all. I was just in town and thought I'd call you up, see how you were doing."

"I'm doing fine. How about you?"

"Fine. Just fine. I'm doing fine too."

There was yet more silence at the other end. It began to lengthen. Butters looked around the cavernous interior of the Hollywood USO. Guys were seated in upholstered chairs reading magazines and newspapers. Across the way a black sailor in dress blues was writing, a letter, Butters assumed, at one of the tables. A notice board beside the bank of phones said there would be a "Servicemen's Seder" at the Jewish Community Center in Pasadena on Thursday. Butters wondered briefly what a seder was.

"Say," he said, breaking the silence (it finally having occurred to him that Phyllis Beardsley didn't intend to), "you didn't happen to be watching TV this afternoon, did you?"

"The idiot box?" Phyllis Beardsley said. "No, I didn't. I'm not in the habit of watching afternoon television, actually—why?"

"Well, you might've seen yours truly if you had. I was on TV!"

"You were, huh? Good for you."

"Yeah. It was this talk show—for housewives. They picked me out of the audience to ask a question."

"What was the question?"

"I forget. Something about, didn't they think it was time for the men to be considered."

"Considered for what?"

"I forget. It was pretty boring."

"Sounds like it."

Butters became aware that he'd been squeezing the receiver. It was slippery in his hand. He loosened his grip. "Listen," he said, "I was wondering if I might come over for a while. What would you think about that?"

"Come over? Here?"

"Yeah. To your place. Or I could meet you somewhere— how about that?"

Silence. "I don't think so. I'm sorry. I've got other plans."

"I was thinking just for an hour or so," Butters said, pressing on. "I'd leave any time you said to. I wouldn't even have to come inside. We could sit out on the steps."

"Steps? What are you talking about? What steps? I'm on the third floor."

"Well, anywhere then. I don't care. Is there a curb? We could sit on the curb. I'd just like to talk to somebody. Somebody that's not in the fucking—excuse me, I didn't mean to say that—not in the Marine Corps—"

He was aware that he was begging, but he didn't seem to be able to stop. It was strange.

"—The thing is, I haven't talked to anybody in so long I'm worried I've forgotten how. If you'd just let me come over for a little while—just thirty minutes—you'd be doing me a big favor. Who knows? You might even be saving my life."

There was another long pause at the other end. Then, "Listen," Phyllis Beardsley said, "I'm going to hang up now. This is getting much too weird. Please don't call here again."

"No!" Butters all but shouted. "Please! Don't hang up. Let's just talk on the phone then, about anything. You pick it. I'm a pretty good conversationalist once you get me started. Really. I'm not dumb. What would you like to talk about? Movies? Sports? Politics? The weather? Pick a subject, any subject. I'll betcha you can't—"

The line suddenly went dead.

Butters looked at the receiver in his hand. It was slick with perspiration. He looked around the big room. The elderly woman behind the reception counter had been peering his way, he saw, but she averted her gaze before their eyes could meet. Had he been talking too loud? Had she heard what he'd said? What *had* he said? He couldn't remember, didn't want to.

He hung up the phone and walked quickly out of the USO.

Now it was much later, past sundown, and he was seated in a bar off La Cienega sipping his third (or was it his fourth?) scotch and water and thinking about the events of a long and dismal day. In the hours since his unsuccessful phone call to Phyllis

Hooray for Hollywood

Beardsley, not much had happened. He'd window shopped some more, considered and rejected taking in a movie at the Pantages (*The Bridge on the River Kwai*, which looked pretty good, but who wanted to watch a prisoner-of-war flick?), had another cheeseburger and more fries at the Bob's Big Boy on Vine, and eventually, utterly at loose ends, circled back to the USO, where he'd sat in one of the leather chairs and read months-old copies of *Sports Illustrated* until his eyes glazed over. Toward sundown, in a fit of desperation, he'd taken an ill-advised (because he knew exactly what to expect) bus ride out to Santa Monica Pier. Sure enough, Santa Monica Pier hadn't changed. It still stuck out into the Pacific, still sagged under the weight of the same number of souvenir and junk-food stands. He'd watched the couples on the amusement park rides for a while, ogled a pair of swimsuited girls on the littered and darkening beach, had a beer and a chili dog, and come on back to Hollywood, where at least there were some bars, and a man could sit down.

The bar he was in was called The Office. Butters liked that because he got it. (Guy could call home, tell his wife, "Looks like I'll be a little late tonight, dear, I'm stuck at The Office.") There was a sign up over the entryway that said, "Work Is the Curse of the Drinking Classes." Butters like that too, recognized it as an inversion of a famous saying by someone—Freud? Marx? Billy Graham?

He'd had the place to himself for the first hour or so, just him and the bartender, but a few minutes ago, another guy had come in and sat down a couple of stools away. Butters eyed the newcomer now in the mirror running behind the bar. He was a handsome devil, older, maybe in his mid-thirties. Butters thought he looked a little like Robert Mitchum.

Oops, the guy caught Butters staring at him in the mirror. He raised his glass to Butters and grinned, lopsidedly, Mitchum-like.

"*Salud.*"

Butters raised his own glass. "*Salud.*" (What was that, Spanish?)

Now the guy was studying *him* in the mirror, Butters saw.

"Hooray for Hollywood," the guy said suddenly. "Right?"

"Yeah, right," Butters said. "Hooray for the whole fucking state, if you ask me."

The guy laughed. "Do I detect a note of bitterness?"

"Nah," Butters said. "Just boredom."

"Marines, huh?" the guy said, taking in his uniform. "Where you from?"

"Texas."

"What part?"

"East Texas."

"What's the town?"

"It's just a little wide spot in the road. You wouldn't of heard of it."

"Try me and see."

Butters told him the town.

"Is that near Nacogdoches?"

"Yeah, about forty miles north of there. Why? You know somebody in Nacogdoches?

"One of my waist-gunners was from there. Tall, lanky kid named MacDougall. Everyone called him 'Abner'."

"Waist-gunners?"

"Yeah, and my bombardier was from El Paso."

Turned out the guy had been a bomber pilot in World War Two. B-17's over Germany, and all that. Butters didn't want to believe him at first, he looked too young, but the guy whipped out his wallet and showed him his old service ID. "First Lt. John R. Dancer," it said underneath a picture of a good-looking fellow in a fleece-lined flight jacket and a jaunty visored cap. The man in the picture was clearly a younger version of the one sitting there beside him: same chin, same eyes, same everything. Butters was impressed. Bomber pilots were some heavyweight studs. Everybody knew that. Something was bothering him, though.

"Why'd they call the guy 'Abner'?" he said. (He thought he knew.) "Was that his name?"

"No, his real name was Lowell, as I remember."

"So why'd they call him 'Abner' then?" Butters said, pressing it.

"Oh, you know—Li'l Abner, Dogpatch, and all that."

"Yeah, that's what I figured," Butters said. "Just another hayseed, huh? Just another East Texas hick."

The man looked at Butters. His Robert-Mitchum features softened. "Hey, come on, Tex," he said, "don't get your feelings hurt. Nobody meant anything by it. Besides, it was a long time ago."

"My name's not 'Tex'," Butters said. "It's Don."

The man looked at his glass. "I'm sorry, Don," he said. "Here, let me buy you a drink."

Butters let him, and he did.

Former Army Air Corps First Lt. John R. ("Call me Jack") Dancer bought current Marine Cpl. Donald J. Butters a drink, and then another one, and then another after that. And the two of them sat there side by side (after Butters shifted over a stool) throughout the rest of the evening, just a couple of late-night strangers in a bar, with service to their country—and maybe a little loneliness—their only bond. But as they sipped their scotch-and-waters (Jack's drink too) and talked, and now and again laughed out loud, anyone watching might have thought, despite the age difference, and the fact that one was in uniform, the other not, that they had known each other for a good long while—might even have thought they were old friends.

"Hey, Jack," Butters said at one point (he'd just remembered something). "You didn't by any chance happen to be watching TV this afternoon, did you?"

"Television?" Jack said. "No, why?"

"I was on there," Butters said. "On the idiot box. Me!"

"Yeah?" Jack said. "Doing what?"

"It was this talk show," Butters said. "That's why I'm in uniform, not civvies. They bussed a bunch of us in from Twentynine Palms to be in the audience, and this guy comes up to me before the show and asks me if I'd like to ask the people onstage a question. So I did it. Right there on TV!"

"Why'd he pick you?"

"I don't know. He just did."

"I think I know why."

"Why?"

"You *look* like a marine. Big, blond, good shoulders. They wanted someone who represented the finest traditions of the Corps."

"Bullshit," Butters said, embarrassed.

"Someone who exemplified the courage and the high moral fiber of America's fighting men."

"Bullshit," Butters said again.

"Someone who'd set their viewers' hearts aquiver."

"Bullshit."

"Also," Jack said, "they probably couldn't afford John Wayne."

Butters laughed. He liked Jack's sense of humor. Jack could be a pretty witty guy.

"What was the question?" Jack said.

"Huh?"

"The question. You said the guy asked you to ask a question."

"Oh," Butters said. "I don't remember now. Something about the man of the house, or some goddamn thing. It didn't make a lotta sense to me. The whole show was pretty dumb if you want to know the truth about it."

"'The man of the house'?"

"Yeah. Something like that."

"The man of the house what? How was that a question?"

"I don't remember. I'm drawing a blank."

"What was the show about?"

"Neighbors."

"Neighbors?"

"Yeah. There was this minister, and this psychiatrist, and a couple of women—I don't know what the hell they did—and they were all talking about neighbors, and being nice to one another, and shit like that."

"What's this show called?"

"*Reach out, LA?*"

"Never heard of it. What time's it on?"

"One o'clock?"

"What channel?"

"Beats me."

"Was it some kind of Christian broadcast thing?"

"Coulda been."

They were silent a moment.

"The man of the house, huh?"

"Yeah…" Butters said. "The man of the house."

"Was that you? Were you the man of the house? You look like you could be the man of someone's house."

Butters laughed. "Who the hell knows? Maybe so. Maybe I was the man of the house and didn't even know it!"

They both laughed at that.

The bar had begun to fill up sometime after eleven, and Butters was surprised to see that Jack knew most of the people who came in. They all seemed to like and admire him too. Turned out he was a neighborhood businessman—owned a commercial photography shop just a couple of blocks away—and many of the people who came in were also area residents who either had business dealings with him or knew him in connection with some social or civic activity. Butters got the impression that he'd somehow stumbled into a tight little community of artisans and businessfolk there in the vast anonymous sprawl of Greater LA, a little enclave of friendliness and familiarity in the midst of its opposite. Some of the newcomers were women too, good-looking ones, and several of these were very friendly with Jack.

By midnight the atmosphere inside the bar had taken on a truly festive tone, and Butters, who'd drunk about a gallon of scotch by then but for some reason still wasn't drunk, began to realize that, for the first time in a very long while, he was actually having *fun*! There was a great deal of laughter and joking up and down the bar, and people were letting him in on it, including him in their conversations, asking his opinion about things. Even the women, when he happened to meet their eyes, smiled at him. And one of them, a pretty brunette, appropriated his garrison cap and wore it all around the bar for a while.

But then something happened that changed everything.

Jack, who'd been acting a little tipsy for some time now, had gone off to the head at one point. And when he came back, he and Butters resumed a conversation they'd been having before, about Jack's studio. Jack had been telling him how it was laid out and all—where the darkrooms were, and the little kitchenette, and the cot he sometimes slept on in back—and they'd more or less agreed that the next time he was in town, Butters, who had expressed a mild interest in photography himself, could maybe swing by the place and Jack would give him a tour. Then they'd discussed the idea a bit further, and Jack had suddenly said, hey, what the heck, why didn't they go do it that very evening, after the bar closed? So then they'd talked about this some, and finally Butters had said, well, sure, why not, sounded like fun to him (maybe there'd be some sexy pictures!)—and it was right about then that he suddenly felt something on his thigh.

A hand. Jack's hand.

Butters didn't know what to make of it at first. Nothing like this had ever happened to him before. Never in his life had anyone he'd been talking to in a bar—a *man*—placed a hand on his thigh. He'd heard all the stories, of course, and knew how you were supposed to handle situations like this, but, still, when it happened to you—a man's hand! right there on his thigh!—it was pretty amazing and took some getting used to.

He turned to look at Jack and saw that Jack was looking at him too. There was a soft, vulnerable, *pleading* expression on Jack's face. Gone was the Robert Mitchum resemblance. He looked as if he might cry.

Butters faced back to the front. The hand was still down there, burning into his thigh. He gazed at himself in the bar's mirror. Was that really *him* sitting there beside that man? It all seemed vaguely unreal, like a scene in a movie. He tried to think, concentrate, but it wasn't easy. He wished he hadn't had so much to drink. He took a deep breath. Then another one. The night bartender was nearby, rinsing some glasses. His name was Vic. He and Jack had bantered back and forth frequently throughout the evening and it was clear that they knew each other pretty well. Butters called him over.

"Hey, Vic," he said (he could feel Jack's hand down there, kneading a little now, massaging). "This guy here"—meaning Jack— "you and him are pretty tight, are you?"

Vic had a glass in his hand, was drying it with a towel. He looked from Butters to Jack and back again, grinning. "Yeah, I'd say so." He had an expectant expression on his face, like a man waiting for a punch line. "Why?"

"Well, guess what?" Butters said.

Vic's expression didn't change. "What?"

"He's got his hand on my leg."

The hand left his leg instantly.

Vic's expression slowly changed. He quit drying the glass. "Yeah?"

"Yeah," Butters said. He turned to face Jack again. And it was funny because everything seemed to be in slow-motion now, very *much* like a scene in a movie. There sat Jack, with a stricken look on his face—fear? disbelief?—and here he, Butters, sat, looking poor Jack square in the eye and saying, "...so if you know him so well, Vic, how come you didn't warn me he was *queer?*"

And, wow, what a reaction that got!

With a little cry of anguish, a whimper almost, Jack was off his barstool and out the front door. Just like that—gone! No slow motion there! Butters had never *seen* anyone move so fast. It gave him a tremendous sense of power. He looked around the bar. He had everyone's attention now. They were all watching him, some with their mouths hanging open, their drink glasses poised in mid-air.

"Yeah, Vic," he continued. (He couldn't disappoint them, could he?) "Seems like you might've warned me or something before you let the guy start feeling me up in your bar. You let all your customers get pawed like that? Is that the kind of place this is? (He was gazing around the room now, the object of all eyes. *He* was Mitchum! This was his big scene!) "I've got lots of buddies out at Twentynine Palms, you know, lots of real good pals. And I might just have to tell them about this place when I get back. And you know what, Vic? They just might decide to come down here and rearrange your furniture for you. Know what I mean? They just might decide to take this place apart, stick by stick. Goddamn *homo* joint. Goddamn *fairy* hangout."

He stood up, took his wallet out of his back pocket and removed a five-dollar bill, the last of his meal money from the TV people. He slapped it on the bar. It meant that he was broke now, that he'd have to hitchhike back out to Twentynine Palms tomorrow, but it seemed like a gesture worth making.

"Here," he growled in his best Mitchum voice. "Keep the change. Split it with your pansy friends."

And with that, he turned and walked out into the late-night air of Greater Los Angeles, a solitary figure, very much alone, but for the moment at least a young man on top of things—a star!

Three Hundred and Twenty-Six Jackrabbits

It was a plan hatched over late-night porkburgers down at Neely's Brown Pig. In the spring of that year, with high school graduation just weeks away, two other boys and I took it into our heads to drive all the way to California from East Texas to see what we could do about improving the brand of football played out there. There was a junior college in El Centro whose coach, we'd been reliably informed, was aching to get his hands on some genuine Texas athletes. We had no trouble believing this. After all, everyone knew Texas high schools produced the finest football players on earth, didn't they? *Didn't they?*

The distance from Moffit, Texas, to El Centro, California, was roughly fifteen hundred miles, and we figured we could make it in two days driving straight through. So, allowing two days for the return trip and three days for us to check the place out and dazzle those Californians with our skills, we estimated we'd be gone a week, which would get us back home just in time for the Senior

Day picnic over at Tyler State Park. We didn't want to miss that.

The members of the student body we'd shared our plans with were equally divided in their response. Some thought we were pretty dashing fellows, others thought we were nuts. There was no such division of opinion among the high school faculty and administration, however. They were unanimous in viewing our announced intention as the absolute pinnacle of harebrained irresponsibility.

Nevertheless, we roared out of Moffit on a Wednesday morning in the last week of April, bound for the Golden State. Behind the wheel was a boy named Marion Morgan. It was his car, a spanking new "sungold" Chevrolet Bel Air convertible, purchased with his mustering out pay from the paratroopers. Marion, having quit school in the tenth grade, had never actually played organized football himself, but he wanted to. It was he who had inflamed us with his reports, over porkburgers down at Neely's, of the California coach looking for players. A Navy friend had put him onto him, he said.

Up front with Marion on that getaway morning was Vernon Wells, maybe my best friend in high school and a one-hundred-and-fifty-five-pound scatback on our high school team, the Mustangs. Vernon's older sister Dolly, a softie who worked for the gas company, had loaned him twenty dollars for the trip, which had Vernon feeling fairly well set up.

I was lolling in the backseat with a lot of game jerseys and athletic socks—our wardrobe for the trip—that we'd borrowed from the stock of a boy named Tubby Mitchell, and with three cans of game film we'd talked Coach C.C. ("Chili") Gillespie into letting us take along as evidence of our prowess. We had also loaded up on such delicacies as Tom's Toasted Peanuts and Hostess chocolate cupcakes, and I had those back there with me too, in a big paper sack.

Longview, Gladewater, Hawkins, Mineola, Grand Saline, Wills Point, Terrell, Dallas. These were the days before the

Interstate system when travel to the West Coast from where we lived was accomplished via U.S. Highway 80, and travelers were obliged to pass through every city and town along the way. Grand Prairie, Arlington, Fort Worth, Weatherford, Ranger, Cisco, Abilene. By mid-afternoon of that first day, we had covered three-hundred miles and only had six hundred more to go to get us out of Texas.

"You saw me crying in the cha-a-pel...," sang June Valli on Marion's car radio. Sang it, that is, until Vernon, impatient with this sob-sister stuff, spun the dial and found *"Take my hand, I'm a stranger in Paradise..."* as rendered by Tony Bennett, which seemed only marginally better. Where was Hank Williams? Where was the good stuff?

By sundown we'd found it on a station out of Del Rio, and "Your Cheatin' Heart" filled the interior of the Chevy now that we'd put the top up. This was some car, I had long ago decided. It still had that new-car smell, and its naugahyde upholstery seemed to me the very last word in contemporary luxury. Truth to tell, it was probably as much the prospect of riding in this car as it was the end-goal of playing football out in California that had launched us, Vernon and I anyway, on this cross-country trip in the first place.

"Who needs one?" I called from the backseat, where I'd been acting as bartender all afternoon long. We had bought three six-packs of beer at the last "package store" in Tarrant County to see us through the "dry" counties ahead, and by nightfall, we had just about worked our way through all three. Amazing how much beer you can hold when you're seventeen.

By midnight, I was driving, and Marion was in the backseat, trying to sleep. We were west of Odessa by then, and Vernon and I were whiling away the miles by counting jackrabbits as they raced across the road in front of our headlights.

"Hunnerd and two," said Vernon. And a few moments later, "Hunnerd and three."

"You think so?" I challenged. "That looked like something else to me."

"Shit. What else is there?"

"You're right. Hunnerd and three."

As dawn broke, we were working our way stoplight by stoplight through dusty downtown El Paso. The city was asleep. Not even a service station was open. Not even, that we could see, an all-night café. Suddenly, however, a police car emerged out of nowhere, its siren wailing, and pulled up behind us at a red light. Two officers got out and approached us. They ordered us out of the car, and we did as they said. Marion, who had been snoring away, came out of the backseat amid a clatter of empty beer cans. The policemen spread-eagled us over the hood of the Chevy, patted us down, then ordered us to follow them to the station just two blocks away.

There, we were booked, had our belts and shoelaces taken away, and were marched upstairs to a large metal holding cell. All of this took place in seemingly no time at all. One minute, we were winging our way to California free as the breeze, and the next, we were sitting in a big iron cage in the El Paso jail.

I was mortified. What was my widowed mother going to think? She hadn't wanted me to make this fool trip in the first place; she'd tried to talk me out of it, but I was seventeen and a football hero and had long since quit listening to her.

Why were we in the El Paso jail? Well, it seems there had been a burglary back home in Moffit. It had happened shortly before we left town. Someone had broken into Tubby Mitchell's bedroom and stolen his collection of silver dollars, coins he was saving to buy an engagement ring for his sweetheart, Marsha Rae Swearingen. This was the same Tubby Mitchell from whom we'd borrowed the jerseys and socks we were now wearing, of course, but he knew about that land had said we could. And, okay, there hadn't been anybody home at his place when we went out there, but we hadn't stolen his damn money. At least,

I didn't think we had. I looked at Vernon. He looked at me. We both looked at Marion. Everyone protested his innocence.

Meanwhile, though, there we sat in the El Paso Jail. Minutes passed, an hour. The cell had another occupant besides us. It was a Mexican-appearing fellow in his mid-twenties, good-looking in a slicked down, Mexican sort of way. He watched us and grinned, giving me the impression he had been there before. After a while, he moved to the front of the cell and began a conversation, through a gap in the metal flooring, with some women in the cell directly below us. The talk was in Spanish. There was an amount of bantering back and forth, incomprehensible to us, then he broke out a long piece of string and dangled it through the gap, down to the other cell. A moment later, he brought it carefully back up and, lo and behold, there was a sandwich attached to the other end. As he sat there eating it, he saw us watching him and grinned again.

"Tiene hambre?" he said, and when we just stared blankly at him, "Joo hongry?"

We admitted that we were, and before long, the Mexican was fishing below for sandwiches for us all. They were just baloney on white bread, but they tasted pretty good after all the peanuts and beef jerky we'd been eating.

"Who are those women down there?" Marion asked our benefactor.

"Putas," he said. "Whores." He pronounced it "oars."

Our interest, already avid, quickened.

"Do you know any of them?" Vernon said.

"Si," the Mexican said. *"Todas. Son mis amigas."*

"Can you fix us up with 'em?" Vernon said.

"Tiene dinero?" the Mexican said. "Joo got money?"

"Some," Vernon said, turning cagey

"How much you got?"

"Enough."

"Let me see."

Vernon reached for his wallet and, finding nothing back there, forced us all to recall that these too had been confiscated, along with our belts and shoelaces.

"Shit," Vernon said. "The cops took it."

The Mexican grinned. "Too bad," he said. *"Pobrecito."*

Our whorish fantasies evaporated in the face of this renewed realization of where we were, what we were doing there, and soon a sort of silent funk had settled over the jail cell. Another hour passed. Then another. What was going on? Was this it? Were they planning to keep us here indefinitely? I began to have visions of myself as a convict, a jailbird. No more football. No more Dairy Queen hot-fudge sundaes. No more Jolene Tierney in the backseat of mother's car at the Fox Drive-in.

By mid-afternoon, the gloom was thick where we were. The Mexican had retreated to his own corner of the cell and was playing solitaire with a deck of cards he'd produced from somewhere. The rest of us had long since run out of things to say to each other. Vernon tried to sleep. Marion had a shoe and sock off and was picking at his toenails. I sat with my arms folded, trying to keep my mind from racing. No more Jolene Tierney!

Suddenly, all unannounced, someone was standing at the cell door. It was our jailer. He unlocked the door with his key and motioned us out.

"Okay," he said. "Let's go."

He didn't have to ask us twice. We scrambled up off the hard metal deck and hurried out after him. Marion didn't even bother to put his shoe and sock back on, just carried them in his hand.

"Adios, muchachos," the Mexican said, looking up from his cards. *"Buen viaje."*

Downstairs, we were given back our belts and shoelaces, along with the rest of our personal belongings, and told we were free to go. Apparently, there had been a wire from the sheriff's department back home saying we were no longer suspects. This was the best news I had had in my entire life. I moved about the room shaking hands with anyone who would shake hands with me. "Thank you," I said. "Thank you, thank you." And moments later we were standing outside in the hot El Paso sunlight, three happy travelers, grateful to be reprieved.

By the time we reached Las Cruces, New Mexico, however, less than an hour away, our brief stopover in the El Paso pokey had been transformed into a real-life adventure, starring us.

"Did you see how big that Mexican's eyes got when I reached for my wallet?" Vernon said. "I think he thought I had a knife."

"I was worried *he* had one," I said. "He seemed to have everything else."

"He could've been a stoolie, you know," said Marion, our elder, giving us the benefit of his wisdom and experience. "Sometimes they do that. Put a stool pigeon in with you to see if you'll say something, give yourself away."

"Damn. You reckon?"

We'd never thought of that.

"He did seem awful shifty."

"It's pretty standard in some of these lockups," Marion said. "Especially the tougher ones, and the El Paso Jail's supposed to be one of the toughest in the country."

"Really? Who says?"

"Everybody. I heard some guys talking about it once at Fort Bragg."

"Toughest in the *coun*try?"

"One of the toughest."

We thought about this. The toughest in the country and we were there. We talked about it for a while longer, massaging it, milking it. Then, changing the subject, Marion said, "Goddamn that Tubby Mitchell. He's cost us half a day's travel. We oughta stomp his ass when we get home. Y'all agree?"

"Damn straight."

"Fuckin' A. His ass is grass, and we're the lawnmower."

And we continued on in this vein for a while: treacherous Tubby Mitchell, and the retribution that awaited him when we got home for having messed with three veterans of the El Paso Jail.

By nightfall, though, it was back to counting jackrabbits.

One hundred and forty-seven...one hundred and forty-eight...one hundred and forty-nine... If we'd thought West Texas was empty, that was before we tried crossing New Mexico and Arizona, where it was sixty miles between towns and the towns—Lordsburg, Deming, Willcox, Benson—were nothing but gas stations with a trading post anyway, and the only radio stations we could pick up were either Gospel or Spanish-language. *One hundred and sixty-three...one hundred and sixty-four...one hundred and sixty-five....*

By dawn, however, we were approaching the California border, with our destination less than a hundred miles away, and the air of excitement inside the Chevy was palpable. We'd made it! Our long trip was almost over, an accomplishment in itself. They knew we were coming too, were expecting us. Marion's friend, the Navy man, had talked by telephone with the coach and we had his, the coach's, address for when we got to town. Now it was just a matter of chewing up the remaining few miles in this excellent car and then wallowing in all the attention we knew awaited us.

Marion was asleep in back again. Vernon was driving, and he and I had been discussing what kind of scholarships we expected these people to offer us. As Texas high school footballers, we were connoisseurs of the various types of college athletic scholarships available; it was something we had been talking about since the ninth grade.

"Well, you can do what you want to," Vernon said finally, "but me, I'm holding out for a full ride. I wouldn't feel right settling for anything less."

The "full ride" was the holy grail of athletic scholarships, the gold standard. It consisted of room, board, tuition, and books, plus a negotiated amount of "laundry money" that was paid out in cash and was said to vary greatly from school to school, with the big Southwest Conference colleges—Texas, Baylor, SMU, and so on—offering the most.

"How about laundry money?" I said. "What do you think's fair?"

"Thirty dollars a week?" Vernon said. "I think I could get by on thirty a week. How about you?"

I mulled it over, giving careful consideration to what it was we were prepared to do for these people, the glory we were prepared to bring them.

"I don't know," I said. "Sounds a little low to me."

"Forty?" Vernon said.

"Forty sounds more like it."

"Okay, forty it is then," Vernon said. "Let's make a pact. We don't settle for anything less than a full ride and forty a week."

We shook on it, right there in the front seat of Marion Morgan's Chevy Bel Air convertible, doing sixty miles an hour on U.S. Highway 80. We would play ball for El Centro Junior College, but we wouldn't sell ourselves cheaply. We owed it to ourselves not to. We owed it to Texas.

"Welcome to California" the big sign just beyond Yuma had said about an hour ago, and now, almost before we knew it, we were approaching the outskirts of El Centro. It was not as I'd pictured it. Although you could see on a map that it was inland, not one of the fabled coastal cities such as San Francisco or San Diego, still, this was California—land of glamour and enchantment, home of movie stars, hot rods, surfers—and one had certain mental images, all of which El Centro fell considerably short of.

It was just another dusty little western town. Agriculture, it turned out, was the main activity around there, thus accounting for all the irrigation ditches we'd been passing lately. The commercial architecture was a bit more Spanish than you might find in East Texas, but otherwise, it looked not unlike Moffit, and it was about the same size.

The address we'd been given turned out to be right downtown, at a corner of the main intersection. The man we were looking for, the coach, was named Bud Hollis, but the building occupying the spot where we expected to find his house was a commercial, not a residential, one, with street-level shops—closed at that hour of the morning—under an arcade. There was an exposed stairway mid-building, though, and after some hesitation, we took this up to the second floor where we confronted, of all things, a large, open-air swimming pool. A sign announced that we'd arrived at the "Civic Natatorium" and I had no idea what that meant. *Natatorium?* A fellow in gym shorts and a tank top was raking the pool with the help of a long pole, however, and we approached him and asked if he knew where we could find Bud Hollis.

He was Bud Hollis. Turned out he managed the swimming pool in the off-season as a way to supplement his income from coaching out at the junior college. He and his wife and two little kids had an apartment up there overlooking the pool. He seemed like a thoroughly nice man, very open, very genial, and, best of all, he was plainly glad to see us. He had been contacted by the Navy man, did know we were coming, and had sort of expected us last night. We apologized for the delayed arrival but didn't tell him what had caused it.

"Have you had breakfast?" he said

And soon we were sitting at the dining table up in the apartment, and Coach Hollis' pretty wife was scurrying about whipping up scrambled eggs and frying sausage patties for us. The Hollises' young son was there with us, being fed before going off to school, and at one point he looked up at me and said, "Are you gonna play football for my Dad?"

I smiled down at the lad, and in my most magnanimous fashion allowed that "We might."

This brought smiles all around the table, and we sat there eating and chatting, warmed by the glow of possibility. Coach Hollis asked us a number of questions about the high school football program back home; he seemed especially interested in the game films we told him we had brought. Apparently, the idea of filming one's games for instructional purposes was a technological breakthrough that hadn't yet reached California (which might have seemed ironic to us if we'd thought about it, California being home to the movie capital and all, but we didn't).

"After you're done eating," the coach said, "I'll take you over to the campus and show you around. There's a photographer coming at ten, or whenever I call him, and I've got a couple of our current players I want you to meet that'll be joining us too. Maybe we can all sit down together this afternoon and look at those game films."

A *photographer?* They were going to take our picture? This was beginning to sound like the Big Time. This was Southwest Conference stuff. This was SMU and Baylor and the Texas Longhorns!

"What kind of photographer?" Vernon said, trying to sound nonchalant.

"Fella from the newspaper," the coach said. "He knows you're coming."

"The *news*paper?"

"Yep."

"You're gonna put us in the newspaper?"

"I thought we would."

Vernon and I looked at each other. We were grinning from ear to ear. Marion seemed slightly less pleased, and I got the impression that he had never had his picture appear much of anywhere, except maybe in the "Our Boys in the Service" section of the paper back home. But Vernon and I knew the value of publicity for an athlete. Having your picture in the paper the day after a game, especially if it was an action shot, was how you created an image for yourself. We knew this because we'd already had our picture in the local paper a time or two and because we had been looking at such pictures of others—Doak Walker, Bobby Layne, Kyle Rote—since before we were old enough to read.

And, sure enough, a couple of hours later there we were out at El Centro Junior College, standing under the goalposts in the football stadium, having our picture taken by a photographer from the El Centro newspaper. Not only that, we were having it taken in full football uniform (except for the shoes)—the colorful red and black silks of the El Centro Red Devils, which Coach Hollis had had us change into over in the locker room. The picture, a two-column shot of the three of us, from the knees up, would appear in the paper the next morning above a caption identifying us as "Texas Athletes Here to Help ECJC."

After the picture-taking session, we changed back into our street clothes—jeans and jerseys—and the coach took us over to his "office" in the school gym. It was really just a desk and some chairs in one of the equipment rooms, and we sat there for a while among the medicine balls and tumbling mats waiting for the two current ECJC players, who were to be our hosts for the weekend, we'd learned, to show up. Eventually, they did.

Their names were Billy Pyle and Kay Hargrove, and they were impressive physical specimens. They seemed much older than we were, more "mature," and I was suddenly embarrassed for Marion in particular, who, though himself older than Vernon and I, had just recently cut a very poor figure in his ECJC football uniform. Vernon and I had had to help him with his shoulder pads, for one thing; he'd tried to put them on backward. And then, when we did get him properly outfitted, his painfully thin bowlegs had been a pitiful sight to see. I couldn't help wondering what Coach Hollis must think. In uniform, Marion simply did not look like a football player.

But even in their street clothes, Billy Pyle and Kay Hargrove most emphatically did. Big, wide-shouldered, and well-muscled, they carried themselves with the looseness and grace that good athletes have. Billy had been a halfback on the past year's team, we learned, and Kay, who was somewhat stockier, had been the fullback. Pyle would go on to star for San Diego State College, I would later learn, and Hargrove would eventually play professionally up in Canada. This day, as Coach Hollis introduced us to them, they both seemed genuinely pleased to make our acquaintance. It was something I was already beginning to notice about Californians—their openness, their friendliness, their air of awareness that they were fortunate to be living where they did, instead of wherever it was you lived, and their belief that there was more than enough of whatever it was they thought they had to go around.

After the introductions, Coach Hollis took us all over to the school cafeteria and fed us ("This one's on ECJC.") and then we all trooped back to the equipment room where it was time to view those game films. Pyle and Hargrove seemed as excited about the prospect as Coach Hollis had been.

A projector was set up, and a screen, and soon we were all watching the flickering, black-and-white recreation of last year's game between the Moffit High School Mustangs and the Lufkin High School Panthers. The film had been shot with a single camera perched above the press box at Mustang Stadium, and all the action appeared to be taking place about a quarter of a mile away. There was no such thing as a close-up.

"That's me going off tackle there," I had to say. "Number thirty-one."

And, "Here's Wells on an end sweep—number twenty-two. Watch me take out that tackle pinching down on him."

The three films we had brought along—of the Lufkin, Texarkana, and Longview games—did not include Vernon's and my best performance of the year, which had been in the Kilgore game. For some reason, that footage hadn't been available to us. Coach Gillespie had withheld it out of spite, Vernon and I believed. He had simply been jealous of the fact that we were going out to California and he wasn't, which was pretty childish of him, we thought. Despite this minor setback, though, Vernon and I delivered a spirited running commentary that afternoon on the films we *had* brought:

"This is where we run the kickoff back for a touchdown. That's me leading the interference there."

"Boy, you remember that play, Wells? That's when you and that big fullback really got into it after the whistle. Too bad the film doesn't show it."

"He clipped me, plain as day, and the official wouldn't call it."

"Here's where Eubanks drops the pass that costs us the district championship. He claimed the lights were in his eyes. But he just dropped it."

"He catches that, and it's on to bi-district."

"Oops. Watch this. This is where Mitchell gets clotheslined by their safety on an end-around. Watch the left-hand corner of the screen. He'll come out of nowhere."

On and on we went like this, and the Californians couldn't seem to get enough of it. They were leaning forward in their chairs, the coach too, like nine-year-olds at a Saturday matinee shoot-'em-up. They kept backing the film up to show certain plays over and over again. They seemed utterly fascinated by what we'd brought them. We ended up spending the whole afternoon there in that smelly equipment room watching those jittery, slightly-out-of-focus high school game films. When we finally did emerge from the place, our stock appeared to have gone up considerably with our hosts and, across the way, the sun was dropping low behind the football stadium.

But now it was Friday evening, and we were on our own. A beach party and cookout had been planned for us for Saturday night, we'd learned, and we were supposed to meet back with the coach on Sunday morning to talk business, but Friday had been left open because no one was sure exactly when we were coming. Coach Hollis had put us up in a guest dorm there on the ECJC campus. It was just a bare room with a couple of double-decker bunks, but that was fine with us. It would beat sleeping in the car.

What to do, though, with all this Friday-night free time?

Like most boys growing up in Texas, we were more or less in thrall to Mexico, or at least to the *idea* of Mexico. To us, it was the Land of the Other, the Land of Anything Goes. East Texas in those days was still very much in the grip of the hard-shell Baptists and other no-nonsense sects such as the Church of the Nazarenes, who frowned on even lipstick and dancing. Henderson County, of which Moffit was the county seat, was still "dry." If you wanted to buy so much as a bottle of beer, you had to drive twenty-five miles to next-door Gregg County. But Mexico? Ah, there, a man could be free. There, a man could do anything he was big enough to do, as long as he had the money.

And guess what? El Centro, as it turned out, was only about ten miles from the Mexican border. This was great news to us. We hadn't known that California *had* a Mexican border. Was Baja California part of Mexico? You could have fooled us.

As soon as night fell, we set out for Mexicali, Baja California, Republic of Mexico. All I knew about Mexicali was that Gene Autry had a song about it, "Mexicali Rose," which I had always kind of liked even as I'd had no idea where Mexicali actually was. Once we got there that evening, though, it turned out to be a fairly typical border settlement.

There was a dominant bar and cantina called El León de Oro in the center of town, and we made our way there in some haste. Soon, we were settled at a stage-side table where just yards away from us a desultory floor show—three bored chorus girls in high heels and feathers fronted by a male singer—was winding down. A waiter approached, and we each ordered a beer. The price of beer in pesos turned out to be the equivalent of thirteen U.S. cents, and our spirits, already fairly high, soared.

At these prices, we could drink all night!

Except for us, the place was almost empty, even though this was a Friday night. There were a couple of middle-aged rancher types over at a far table and some dowdy-looking Mexican women at another one, but that was about it. We were the main action as far as paying customers went, and that was fine with us.

Little barefoot kids kept coming through, though, pestering us, cutting into our party time. They tried to sell us chewing gum. They tried to sell us flowers. They tried to sell us rosaries, pocket combs, harmonicas. Each of them had a sad story about how tough things were at home. We found these easy enough to believe just from the looks of them. Vernon finally bought a pair of sunglasses for a dollar and proceeded to put them on and wear them there in the cantina. Marion bought a deck of playing cards with naked women on the backs.

After a while, some younger women and girls came in and sat down at a table nearby. There were five of them. The oldest looked to be in her mid-twenties and the youngest no older than Vernon and me. They all had on shiny, taffeta dresses and high heels and lots of makeup. In the bad light of the cantina, they looked pretty good, especially a couple of the younger ones. They smiled in our direction, and one of them waved at us.

"Hey, did you see that?" Vernon said. "She waved at me."

"I think she likes you," Marion said. "Go over there and talk to her."

"It's those shades," I said. "She thinks you're Tab Hunter."

Vernon had kinky red hair and acne. His eyebrows were almost white.

"You think I should?" he said to Marion. "What would I say?"

"Tell her you're madly in love with her. Tell her you want to marry her."

"Naw, really."

"Tell her you're a rich Texas oilman and you'd like to buy her a drink."

Three Hundred and Twenty-Six Jackrabbits

Vernon looked doubtful. "You think she'd believe me?"

"That you wanted to buy her a drink?"

"No, shithook. That I was a rich Texas oilman."

"Who knows? It's worth a try."

"Tell her you're a hotshot football player here to rescue the fortunes of ECJC," I suggested.

This seemed a bit more plausible to Vernon. He sat, contemplating it. Meanwhile, the girl was still waving at us. A couple of the others were waving now, too. There were also lots of smiles emanating from the other table. I locked eyes with one of the younger girls, but she didn't smile, just sat there appraising me. In the semi-darkness of the cantina, she seemed out of place, a stranger at the party. She was also very pretty.

From out of nowhere—just like those El Paso policemen—a young man materialized. Suddenly, he was at our table, bending over us. He couldn't have been much older than we were.

"You like these girls?" he said. "You want to get to know them better? I can fix you up."

We looked up at him. Where had he come from? He continued to speak to us, rapidly, smoothly. He looked Mexican, but his English was better than ours was. He knew these girls very well, he said. He had gone to school with some of them. They were very clean, very passionate. They knew what a man liked. Five dollars would buy a whole night with one of them, three dollars would buy a "short time." He gazed into our rapt, upturned faces.

"Anyone interested?' he said.

Her name, she told me, was Concepta. We were in a room out back of the cantina. She was the girl who had returned my stare some moments earlier, and I thought I was in love with her already. She had put my three dollars on the washstand in her little room and indicated to me that I should unbutton my jeans. I hesitated. She indicated again, and somewhat impatiently, and, embarrassed, I began to comply.

She took off her shiny, red dress and climbed up on the bed. I took off my jeans and game jersey—number 77—and scrambled after her. There was a little low-watt lamp beside the bed, and she reached for it, then paused.

"*Luz o oscura?*" she said.

"Huh?"

"Lice on, lice off?"

It was a decision I was not prepared to make. I wasn't a virgin—not quite—but all my experience up till then had been in the backseats of cars. This was an issue that had never come up.

"Um, I don't care. You pick it."

"Okay," she said, "lice on," and soon, lights on, we were doing what we'd come there for.

Afterward, on the drive back to El Centro, we compared notes. Vernon's girl was named Maria Elena, he said, and she had a brother in Lubbock who worked in a car wash. I asked him if they did it with the lights on or the lights off and he said off, why? Just wondering, I said. Marion said he hadn't bothered to get his girl's name, but if he ever went back there, he was going to ask for her again because she was a real pro.

"Yeah? What'd she do?"

"Everything."

"Like what?"

"You name it."

"Blow job?"

"Yep."

"Around the world?"

"Yep."

"Corn hole?"

"Yep."

That about exhausted our knowledge of the sexual possibilities, and we weren't even sure about a couple of those. Marion, who was driving, had his wrist draped over the steering wheel and the smile on his face bespoke a man of vast experience. Vaster, at any rate, than Vernon's and mine.

"What else?"

"All of it. The whole shootin' match."

"Well, like what for example?"

Marion just smiled his smile. "If you don't know, I can't tell you."

"Aw, come on, Marion. Sure you can."

"Nope. It wouldn't be right. I might corrupt you."

"Come on, Marion."

"Maybe someday—when you're older."

"Aw, come on."

"Not right now."

"Aw."

Mid-morning of the next day, we were sleeping soundly in the bare dorm room when Billy Pyle and Kay Hargrove showed up and started shaking us awake. Up and at 'em, they said. Rise and shine. It was time to head up to Brawley, where arrangements were already underway for today's cookout and beach party. There was still food and beer to buy, though, and other odds and ends, such as rounding up a few more girls, to attend to. Hargrove had a copy of the local newspaper with him, and he plopped it down in front of us. There, at the top of the second section, was the picture ("Texas Athletes Here To Help ECJC") that had been taken the day before, with me squinting at the camera, Vernon, his chin thrust out, looking militant, and Marion, his thin neck rising from the deep well of his shoulder pads, looking the complete impostor, God love him, that he was.

Brawley, it turned out, was a slightly larger town some fifteen miles to the north of El Centro. It billed itself as the hub city of the Imperial Valley, which the signs told us contained some of the richest farmland on earth. "We Feed the Nation," the signs bragged. And indeed Brawley did seem a step up from El Centro. Cleaner, more prosperous looking, more *Californian.* There were palm trees lining the streets, for instance, and lots of fine, "ranch-style" homes with wide, manicured lawns. Everybody, even the kids, seemed to be driving a brand-new car. Brightly painted hot rods abounded, and suddenly Marion's sungold Chevrolet began to look almost dowdy by comparison. *This*, I started to feel, was it. This was what we'd come for.

"Let's go see Drollinger," Kay Hargrove said. "Find out what's happening." He was in Marion's car with us, giving directions; Pyle was following in another vehicle. We set off in search of "Drollinger."

Surprisingly, Drollinger turned out to be a girl. First name, Pam, and she was gorgeous. I'd never in my life seen anyone that pretty. There wasn't a girl in all of East Texas that pretty. She came out to the curb to greet us, when we pulled up in front of her parents' house in a residential part of Brawley, wearing shorts and a wrinkled tee-shirt. Her figure was remarkable, as was her tan. Now this, indisputably, I thought, was California.

"Hey, Drollinger," Hargrove said. "These are the guys I was telling you about." He introduced us around.

The girl smiled, radiantly, at each of us in turn. It was like headlights being turned on, the sun breaking through clouds.

"Are they treating you okay?" she said. "Are you finding anything to do?"

We said they were treating us fine, we were finding plenty to do—without being too specific—then Hargrove said, "How about it, Drollinger? You going to be able to shake loose?"

"What time you guys heading out?" she said.

"Ricky-tick," Hargrove said. "Soon as we make a couple of pit stops. You talk to Searcy? She coming?"

"She's leaning," the girl said. "I'm supposed to call her. You guys in a sweat? You want to come inside and hang while I buzz her?"

"Gotta split," Hargrove said. "Gotta blow. Give her a ring, though, then you guys can come out together."

I was sitting in the backseat with Vernon, taking in all this snappy California dialog, trying to get used to girls being called by their last names, to everyone, whether male or female, being referred to as "guys."

Billy Pyle had gotten out of the other car by now and sauntered up beside Drollinger. He put an arm around her waist familiarly and said, "Be extra nice to these guys, Drollinger. They're here to save us."

Drollinger looked inside the car and bathed us again with that smile.

"Oh, I hope so," she said.

A short time later, we were driving through the countryside, on our way to a reservoir outside Brawley. It was a mild spring afternoon, with warm breezes rustling in the tall palms overhead. Water gushed and gurgled in the irrigation ditches on either side of the road and out in the fields we passed were bumper crops of lettuce, cantaloupe, and artichokes.

At the reservoir there was a fine sandy beach, and by late afternoon we had the portable grills set up, had the charcoal going, had the chests of iced-down beer firmly planted in the shade of some ocotillo shrubs, had the easy-listening California tunes emanating from someone's battery-operated portable radio (*"Hey there, you with the stars in your eyes…"*) and were well-launched toward an evening of good, clean outdoor fun.

The reservoir sort of reminded me of the lake at Tyler State Park back home. It was about the same size, at any rate, and the water temperature, surprisingly, was about the same. There were twenty or so of us revelers, all told, about half of the number girls. Pyle and Hargrove had supplied swimsuits for Vernon, Marion, and me—we not having thought to bring our own, of course—and in between bouts of beer drinking and tossing one of the several available footballs around on the sand, we had taken an occasional dip in the somewhat chilly water. All the Californians were big swimmers, I saw, men and women alike; they seemed much more at home in the water than we did. There was lots of splashing, head-dunking, and other such horseplay on their part, girls included, as we, meanwhile, more or less squatted in the shallows and watched.

It was also impossible not to notice that the Californians were, without exception, better physical specimens than we were. Their teeth were straighter, and whiter, their complexions clearer, their postures better, and of course they all had great tans. Most of the boys were members of the ECJC football team, and as such were maybe a year or two older than Vernon and me, but they seemed so much bigger, better muscled, more physically mature than us that age alone couldn't account for it.

As for the girls, they were uniformly attractive. Lithe, tawny, and self-confident, they bounded about the beach as if they were born to it, as no doubt they were. There were two or three bikinis in the group, though none of the extreme variety—this was 1954, after all—and Vernon, Marion, and I had trouble keeping our eyes in our heads at times. The California males, of course, didn't even appear to notice that some of these girls were practically naked. For all they seemed to care, the girls could have been wearing nuns' habits.

By nightfall, with the coals dying in the grills and several pounds of hamburger and hot dogs digesting in our collective bellies, we were nestled snugly in the still-warm sand in small groups, having paired off, most of us, with someone of the opposite sex. Lucky me, I had somehow managed to link up with Pam Drollinger, and I was busy telling her all about myself.

"Oh, I don't know," I was saying. "*Arthur Godfrey and Friends*, I guess. That and *Dragnet*. How about you?" I'd already told her what my favorite movies were, and my favorite popular songs.

"Arthur Godfrey?" she said. "Why watch him?"

"I don't know. Habit, I guess. I used to listen to him on the radio." I didn't tell her we only got one television channel, out of Shreveport, Louisiana, in Moffit and that Godfrey was on it.

"What did you think of him firing Julius LaRosa?"

"I thought he deserved it, didn't you? He was getting too big for his britches, if you ask me."

"He's got a pretty voice, though."

"He does. But so does Tony Marvin."

"What's your favorite color?"

"Green."

"Why green?"

"I don't know—because it matches my eyes?"

"Your eyes aren't green."

"Yeah, they are."

"Let me see."

It was getting dark by then, and there was no way she could tell what color my eyes were, but she bent down over me anyway, pretending to examine them, and right at that moment, we heard a voice from out front of us, just a few feet away.

"Drollinger, you dumb bitch, where are you?"

It was Kay Hargrove. He'd been drinking beer all afternoon, more of it, even, than the rest of us, and had been acting grouchy and belligerent for the past couple of hours: throwing the football too hard from too close up, dunking people with a bit too much enthusiasm, and so on. Now he was standing out there in front of Drollinger and me with his fists on his hips and his legs spread apart in the sand.

"Kay," she answered him. "What is it? I'm right here."

"What are you doing down there?"

"Talking. We're discussing the firing of Julius LaRosa. Why?"

"I've been looking for you."

"Well, now you've found me."

"Yeah, now I've found you."

Silence. Drollinger didn't say anything. Hargrove, fists still on hips, stood there glaring down at us.

"Hey there, Kay," I said. "What's up?"

"Keep outta this, Dogpatch," he said. "I'm talking to her."

"Come on now, Kay," Drollinger said soothingly. "What's the matter with you? What's wrong?"

"Nothing's the matter with me. I was looking for you, and now I've found you."

"Yes, now you have. What can I do for you?"

"You can't do shit for me, Drollinger. You can't do a goddamn thing."

"Here now, easy," I said, and started to get up from the sand.

"You stay out of this, hayseed," Hargrove said, "if you don't want your face pushed in. You and your fucking game films."

Hargrove was bigger than me and, as I've indicated, much better muscled. I wasn't eager to tangle with him. Drollinger put her hand on my arm to restrain me, but she needn't have bothered. I wasn't going anywhere.

"Come out here with your fancy bullshit," Hargrove was saying. "You Texas Okies think you're really something, don't you? 'Too bad the film doesn't show it,' 'Back it up, Vernon, let's look at the replay.'"

Drollinger, with a sigh, began to gather up her things. "I'd better go talk with him," she said. "He's had a little too much to drink."

"Can I do anything?" I said, pretending a willingness to intervene that I didn't really have.

"No, you stay here. I'll be back. I just need to talk to him. He gets this way sometimes."

"Yeah, keep your seat, Gomer," Hargrove said. "You might go back to Mount Idy in a meat wagon."

Drollinger went off with him, and I sat there on the sand waiting for her to return. Ten minutes passed, twenty minutes, thirty minutes, but she never came back. Eventually, the party began to break up. People started packing up and heading for their cars. I was still sitting on the sand, waiting, and by then, Vernon and Marion had joined me. Some of the ECJC team members stopped by as they were leaving to tell us it was nice meeting us and they hoped they'd be seeing us in the fall. One of them told me not to worry too much about Hargrove. He was a good guy, he said, he just got kind of mean sometimes when he'd been drinking. On the way back down to El Centro, Vernon—it was just we three Texans in Marion's car now—said to me, "You and that Drollinger were hitting it off pretty good, weren't you? What was it Hargrove came over and said to you?"

"Aw, nothing much. He was mostly talking to her."

"He seemed kinda pissed off."

"Yeah, he was."

"Was he jealous, you think?"

"He kept bringing up those game films of ours like they really upset him or something."

"Well, fuck him then. Just because they never thought to film their own damn games. What kind of rinky-dink operation they running out here anyway?"

"I've been wondering the same thing myself. Did you notice how small that stadium was yesterday? I bet they don't seat seven thousand. Hell, we do better than that back home."

"Yeah, and did you see that press box? It wasn't no bigger than a cowshed. Open at both ends."

"Let's ask Coach Hollis about that tomorrow."

"About what?"

"You know, are they planning on enlarging the stadium, upgrading their press box if we agree to come out here?"

"Good idea. I'll bring it up if you don't. You still holding out for a full ride?"

"Yeah, I won't settle for anything less. How about you, Marion? You still with us?"

"Shit, yes. I ain't taking less than ya'll get. Coming out here was my idea in the first place."

"Okay, it's a deal then—a pact." We all clasped hands. "Full rides or nothing."

Tomorrow was to be our last day in California. We were meeting with the coach for breakfast at his apartment above the swimming pool at eleven o'clock, then heading on back to Texas after that. We still planned to make it back in time for the Senior Day picnic. I was down to my last pair of clean socks, and I suspected from the smell of things that Vernon had already used up his. As we entered the outskirts of El Centro, Marion asked us how much money we had left. I said about seven dollars, and Vernon said about ten. Gasoline was twenty-three cents a gallon, and we'd need about five tankfuls to get us home. Marion did some figuring with his fingers and said we were okay, money was no problem. The clock on the dashboard read ten-thirty.

"In fact," Marion said, "we've got time for another quick run to Mexicali if anyone's interested."

"Dedo."

We were lying on the bed in Concepta's little room out back of the cantina, and she was giving me the Spanish words for the various body parts as I pointed to them.

"Mano. Brazo. Pecho. Estomago." She giggled and slapped at my hand. *"Vaheena. Pierna. Rodilla. Peeay."*

It was after midnight by then, and I had been with her for more than an hour. I was going to be strapped for cash the next day. We'd been discussing our separate plans, hers and mine. She'd like to come to the States, she said, maybe get a job in one of the packing plants around Brawley, or maybe go stay with a cousin of hers in Albuquerque. She couldn't be a whore forever. The pay was okay, but the risks—disease, corrupt cops, a certain criminal element—were too high. Besides, she'd be twenty years old in a couple of years, and her looks would probably start to go. How far was Albuquerque from where I lived? she wanted to know. *"Esta muy lejos?"*

Three Hundred and Twenty-Six Jackrabbits

I told her it was a long way. *Mucho* miles.

"How many?" she asked.

I didn't know. "A lot," I said.

She nodded. "But not *such* a lot?"

"No," I agreed. "Not such a lot."

Did they have *futbol* in Albuquerque? she wanted to know.

Yes, I told her. I was pretty sure they had a college there that had a team.

Might it be possible that I could play for the team in Albuquerque then?

No, I told her, because the team in Albuquerque hadn't offered me a scholarship the way ECJC, I was confident, was about to.

Concepta had trouble with this idea of a scholarship. She couldn't quite grasp it. They gave it to you for school or for the *futbol?* she asked.

"Both," I said.

But how could a scholarship be for playing a game? she wanted to know. Would I be learning the game, studying it?

No, I told her. I already knew the game. That's why they were giving me the scholarship, to play it for them.

They don't know it? she said. *"No lo intienden?"*

They knew it too, I told her. We both knew it.

Then who learns it? she said. Who is the scholar?

I finally gave up trying to explain it to her, just let her accept it for the gringo foolishness it was, and we went back to the business of naming parts.

"Ojo," she said. *"Nariz. Boca. Labios."*

I leaned over to kiss her on the *labios*, and she let me.

I looked down at her. She smiled up at me.

"Te amo," she said a short while later when I asked her to help me phrase what it was I wanted to tell her.

Coach Hollis' wife had prepared another huge meal for us. There were omelettes and bacon, and waffles if we wanted them.

There were sweet rolls and biscuits and several different kinds of jam. There was even something called guava juice, which was supposed to be high in fiber and muscle-building protein.

We showed up at the swimming-pool apartment on time but looking a little the worse for wear. We hadn't got back to the guest dorm until near dawn.

"Dig in, fellas," Coach Hollis said when we were seated at the table. "Don't let it get cold. How about some of this bacon, Vernon?"

Billy Pyle had joined us, but Kay Hargrove wasn't there. The coach said he had something else he had to do and might show up later. Billy whispered to us that he was suffering from a monster hangover.

"How was the cookout?" the coach said. "Did they show you a good time? Bill, did Ramirez and the others show up?"

Pyle said there was a good turnout for the party, lots of people showed up. Nobody mentioned Kay Hargrove's antics.

Marion said, "Pass the biscuits."

Vernon said, "I'll have one of those waffles."

I said, "Guava juice, huh? Not bad. Not bad."

Sometime later, after the dishes had been cleared, Coach Hollis suggested we all go down and sit at one of the poolside tables. "Bill," he said to Pyle, "why don't you stay up here and help Marge with the dishes?"

The three of us followed Coach Hollis out of the apartment and down to the pool, where we sat down with him around one of the metal tables there. It was clear from the coach's expression that the time had come to talk turkey. I put on my game face and so did Vernon.

"Well, fellas," the coach said with no preamble, "what do you think? Have you seen enough? Would you like to come out here and play for us? If you would, we'd love to have you. I think you'd like it around here. It's a good area. The people are steady and God-fearing. The school's fairly new, but I think you can get a pretty good education here, depending on what you want to study. We're big in crop management, soil science, and the like. Have you had a chance to talk it over among yourselves yet?"

Vernon and I looked at each other. Marion looked at both of us. We couldn't decide who ought to speak.

"Um," I began. "What's the setup? What do we get if we do decide to come here? Besides the education, I mean?"

The coach looked at each of us in turn. There was a puzzled expression on his face.

"What do you mean?"

"What kind of scholarships are you offering?"

"Scholarships?"

"Yeah, you know, room, board, tuition—stuff like that. What kind of a deal would you give us?"

"Laundry money," Vernon said, nudging me. "Don't forget the laundry money."

The coach had a funny look on his face. "Wait a second, fellas," he said. "Hold on. There must be some—"

"We was thinking along the lines of a full ride," Marion said, his face showing his pride at having mastered the term.

"Plus laundry money," Vernon insisted. "I myself, personally, would need at least forty dollars a week in laundry money. I can't speak for these others, but that's what I'd need. Forty. Minimum."

"Me too," Marion chimed in. "I ain't taking anything less than he gets."

The coach was shaking his head. "Fellas," he was saying. "Fellas. Whoa. Let's come back down to earth here. There's obviously been a misunderstanding of some kind. We don't offer scholarships at ECJC. We're a *junior* college. The state doesn't allow it. Nobody gets to offer them. We can maybe help you with a part-time job, setting siphon hoses out in the onion fields, or working in a packing plant or something. We help some of the boys that way. But scholarships? No. That's just not a possibility."

We were stunned. Could it be true? Were we hearing this man correctly?

"Not even room and board?" I said.

The coach shook his head.

"Not even tuition and books?" Vernon said.

The coach shook his head again.

"How about the laundry money?" Marion said.

The coach just looked at him.

Silence fell over the little poolside table. Could it be that we had driven fifteen hundred miles and jeopardized our (or at least my) high school graduation for a mirage? A chimera? For something that didn't even exist? The fact of it was just too awful to contemplate. We'd be laughingstocks back home. We'd never hear the end of it. What would we tell people? What could we possibly say?

I turned to Marion. "I thought you said your Navy buddy said—"

Marion turned his palms up. "Hell," he said. "He *did*. He said they were looking for players and they'd give us anything we wanted. That's exactly what he told me. I swear to God."

We looked at the coach.

"What Navy buddy?" he said. "Did he go to school here?"

We looked back at Marion.

"I *think* so," Marion said.

"Is he the fella who called me and said you were coming out?"

"Yeah," Marion said, relieved to have the Navy buddy's existence, at least, confirmed. "Yeah, that's him."

"All he said was that you were coming. He said you played high school ball in Texas and were looking for some place to continue playing. There was no talk about scholarships or anything like that."

We looked at Marion, Vernon and I.

"He didn't say anything to you about scholarships?" Marion

said to the coach. "Not a thing?"

Coach Hollis just shook his head.

Silence descended again on the little poolside table. I looked down into the pale, greenish water just a few feet from where we sat. Overnight, a few thin leaves had blown into it from somewhere and were floating now on the water's surface. The coach was going to have to get his rake out again.

Finally, after what seemed like a very long time, Marion said, "Those part-time jobs. How much would they pay?"

"Goddamn a hunnerd and ninety-two," Vernon said. "Goddamn a hunnerd and ninety-three."

We were back on Highway 80 again, heading east through Arizona at sundown, counting jackrabbits.

The mood in the sungold Chevy was not good. Marion sat hunched over the wheel with Vernon in the seat beside him. I was in the back with the cans of game film that were supposed to make all the difference but hadn't. I was considering throwing the damn things out the window. Marion had quit being defensive by now and had gone on the attack.

"It was y'all's idea as much as it was mine," he said. "And don't try to deny it, Vernon. You about peed in your pants when I said we could take this car."

"I ain't denying anything," Vernon said. "I just wish you'd asked a few more questions first, that's all."

"Like what?"

"Like did they offer fuckin' scholarships out there, for one thing."

"I didn't know nothing about scholarships. What did I know about scholarships? I never even finished the tenth grade."

"Shit. You acted like you did."

"Naw, I didn't."

"Yeah, you did."

"Goddamn a hunnerd and ninety-four," I said.

*

By the time we reached the New Mexico border, I had begun to realize that I was probably never going to see Concepta again, and that had opened up a big hole inside me at right about chest level. Suddenly I missed her badly. Already. Then I also realized I didn't even know her last name.

"Hey," I said to Vernon. "If you were gonna write a letter to somebody in Mexico, how would you go about it? Just address it to such and such and so and so in Mexicali, Mexico?"

"Yeah," Vernon said. "That's what I'd do. Slap a stamp on it."

"How big a stamp?"

"I don't know. Ask the post office."

"Could you just send it to someone's first name, care of a bar, do you think?"

"You could *try*. I don't know what the Mexican mail service is like, but if it's like everything else down there I wouldn't hold my breath till she gets it."

It was a depressing thought, having to rely on the Mexican postal authorities to see to it that a teenaged whore whose last name you didn't even know got a letter from you addressed in care of a bar. It seemed like the longest of long shots. Might as well put it in a bottle and drop it in the Rio Grande, hope it could float upstream.

"Shit," I said.

"Goddamn two hunnerd and thirty-six," said Vernon.

Retracing our route was not nearly as much fun as laying it down in the first place. What had seemed adventurous and exciting before became stale and hum-drum the second time around. By the time we reached El Paso, scene of our earlier, now mythic (in our own minds) police encounter, we had no desire to linger. With the jackrabbit count approaching three hundred and our little corner of East Texas still nine hundred miles away, all we wanted to do was keep going.

"Wonder if that ol' boy's still fishing for baloney sandwiches up there in jail?" was all anyone said.

Outside of Pecos, in a rainstorm, something definitely not a jackrabbit crossed the highway in front of our headlights. It was large and black and moving very fast, with a long, loping gait.

"Hey," I said, "did you see that?"

I was driving now, with Vernon still in the front seat beside me. Marion was snoring in back. It was sometime after midnight.

"Yeah," Vernon said. "What was it?"

"I don't know. It sure as hell wasn't a jackrabbit, though."

"A cat maybe?"

"It was too big for a cat."

"I mean like, you know—a panther?"

I looked over at Vernon. "They don't have panthers around here—do they?"

"I don't know. I didn't think so. Not black ones anyhow. But you're right, it sure as hell wasn't no jackrabbit. That's for sure."

"A panther," I said, playing with the idea. "Damn. You really think that's what it was?"

"I don't know, but if it wasn't, it's the biggest damn house cat *I* ever saw."

I drove on in silence, pondering what we'd just witnessed. It did nothing to lighten my mood. Or Vernon's either, I could tell. A big black cat had crossed our path. At around midnight. Given what all we'd been through, it seemed almost eerily fitting.

Big Spring, Sweetwater, Abilene. Daylight found us re-entering the known world—the part of it, that is, we were more or less accustomed to. By mid-morning, we were on the outskirts of Fort Worth ("Where the West Begins") and could begin to think thoughts of East Texas and home. Vernon was driving, and I was slumped against the window on the passenger side, fighting sleep. Marion was sitting up in the backseat by now, but looking gray-faced like the rest of us and just as out of sorts. We were all exhausted: physically, emotionally, spiritually. Three thousand miles of straight-through driving in a little over six days will take it out of you, even at seventeen.

We'd been discussing what to do—head straight on to Moffit or swing by Tyler State Park as we'd originally planned? The consensus seemed to be to skip Tyler, limp on home, try to forget the whole sorry business. If we went to Tyler, what were we going to say? They were bound to ask us a lot of questions.

We made it through Fort Worth and then Dallas in stony silence. This had become an endurance test, and we were still in danger of failing it. At least we were in the home stretch now, and as we passed through Forney and Terrell and began to get our first whiffs of East Texas, we rallied a little. Soon Wills Point would be coming up, and with it, the beginning of the piney woods. We'd have come in off the plains.

We were still on Highway 80, as we had been so much of the time, going and coming, for days. At Mineola, however, suddenly there was a sign that said Tyler was only twenty miles away, on Highway 69, if we chose to take the turn-off, which was coming up fast.

"Hey, I didn't know Tyler was that close," Vernon said.

It was still seventy-five more miles to Moffit on Highway 80. We had to go through Wood County and Gregg County yet.

"Me neither," I said. "I guess I never noticed that sign before."

"What kind of road is Highway 69?"

"I don't know. Never been on it."

"Think we oughta give it a try?"

"Do you?"

"I asked you first."

"What do you think, Marion?" I said. "You want to give Highway 69 a try?"

"Makes no difference to me," Marion said from the back seat. "I just want to get out of this damn car."

Within thirty minutes, we were pulling into the visitors'

parking lot at Tyler State Park. There sat three big yellow-and-black buses from the Henderson County Independent School District, bold as you please, and like a stray come home to the litter, we nestled Marion's car right up alongside them and parked it. We didn't bother to change clothes or spruce ourselves up or anything, simply headed straight down toward the beach.

The first of our classmates to see us coming got these frozen, astonished looks on their faces. Who were these guys? It was if they thought they recognized us, but then again, they weren't really sure. Somehow, we had been transformed. We were Lewis and Clark. We were Magellan, Christopher Columbus—*Marco Polo!*—returned with news of another, grander world.

They crowded all around us. They wanted to hear, *needed* to. We described for them the wonders of all we had seen—the riches of Cathay, the Hanging Gardens of Babylon, moonlight on the Ganges, Tahiti with its dusky maidens, Kilimanjaro and its snow-capped peak…

Someone said they had heard we were in jail, and yes, we admitted, it was true. Devil's Island, the Chateau D'If, Dannemora and its cold, hard walls, the pitiless cliffs of Sing Sing…None were strangers to us now.

And more, they insisted, tell us more. So we did. Safe on the domesticated sands of Tyler State Park, back among the familiar pines and chokeberry bushes of East Texas, we rambled on and on about forbidden pleasures and riotous nights, about this and that and such and so and a thousand other things.

The silly, inconsequential business of the football scholarships never even came up.